Castles in the Air

by

Baroness Emmuska Orczy

The Echo Library 2006

Published by

The Echo Library

Echo Library
131 High St.
Teddington
Middlesex TW11 8HH

www.echo-library.com

Please report serious faults in the text to complaints@echo-library.com

ISBN 1-40683-583-8

FOREWORD

In presenting this engaging rogue to my readers, I feel that I owe them, if not an apology, at least an explanation for this attempt at enlisting sympathy in favour of a man who has little to recommend him save his own unconscious humour. In very truth my good friend Ratichon is an unblushing liar, thief, a forger—anything you will; his vanity is past belief, his scruples are non-existent. How he escaped a convict settlement it is difficult to imagine, and hard to realize that he died—presumably some years after the event recorded in the last chapter of his autobiography—a respected member of the community, honoured by that same society which should have raised a punitive hand against him. Yet this I believe to be the case. At any rate, in spite of close research in the police records of the period, I can find no mention of Hector Ratichon. "Heureux le peuple qui n'a pas d'histoire" applies, therefore, to him, and we must take it that Fate and his own sorely troubled country dealt lightly with him.

Which brings me back to my attempt at an explanation. If Fate dealt kindly, why not we? Since time immemorial there have been worse scoundrels unhung than Hector Ratichon, and he has the saving grace— which few possess—of unruffled geniality. Buffeted by Fate, sometimes starving, always thirsty, he never complains; and there is all through his autobiography what we might call an "Ah, well!" attitude about his outlook on life. Because of this, and because his very fatuity makes us smile, I feel that he deserves forgiveness and even a certain amount of recognition.

The fragmentary notes, which I have only very slightly modified, came into my hands by a happy chance one dull post-war November morning in Paris, when rain, sleet and the north wind drove me for shelter under the arcades of the Odéon, and a kindly vendor of miscellaneous printed matter and mouldy MSS. allowed me to rummage amongst a load of old papers which he was about to consign to the rubbish heap. I imagine that the notes were set down by the actual person to whom the genial Hector Ratichon recounted the most conspicuous events of his chequered career, and as I turned over the torn and musty pages, which hung together by scraps of mouldy thread, I could not help feeling the humour—aye! and the pathos—of that drabby side of old Paris which was being revealed to me through the medium of this rogue's adventures. And even as, holding the fragments in my hand, I walked home that morning through the rain something of that same quaint personality seemed once more to haunt the dank and dreary streets of the once dazzling Ville Lumière. I seemed to see the shabby bottle-green coat, the nankeen pantaloons, the down-at-heel shoes of this "confidant of Kings"; I could hear his unctuous, self-satisfied laugh, and sensed his furtive footstep whene'er a gendarme came into view. I saw his ruddy, shiny face beaming at me through the sleet and the rain as, like a veritable squire of dames, he minced his steps upon the boulevard, or, like a reckless smuggler, affronted the grave dangers of mountain fastnesses upon the Juras; and I was quite glad to think that a life so full of unconscious humour had not been cut short upon the gallows. And I thought kindly of him, for he had made me smile.

There is nothing fine about him, nothing romantic; nothing in his actions to cause a single thrill to the nerves of the most unsophisticated reader. Therefore, I apologize in that I have not held him up to a just obloquy because of his crimes, and I ask indulgence for his turpitudes because of the laughter which they provoke.

EMMUSKA ORCZY. *Paris, 1921.*

CASTLES IN THE AIR

CHAPTER I

A ROLAND FOR HIS OLIVER

1.

My name is Ratichon—Hector Ratichon, at your service, and I make so bold as to say that not even my worst enemy would think of minimizing the value of my services to the State. For twenty years now have I placed my powers at the disposal of my country: I have served the Republic, and was confidential agent to Citizen Robespierre; I have served the Empire, and was secret factotum to our great Napoléon; I have served King Louis—with a brief interval of one hundred days— for the past two years, and I can only repeat that no one, in the whole of France, has been so useful or so zealous in tracking criminals, nosing out conspiracies, or denouncing traitors as I have been.

And yet you see me a poor man to this day: there has been a persistently malignant Fate which has worked against me all these years, and would—but for a happy circumstance of which I hope anon to tell you—have left me just as I was, in the matter of fortune, when I first came to Paris and set up in business as a volunteer police agent at No, 96 Rue Daunou.

My apartment in those days consisted of an antechamber, an outer office where, if need be, a dozen clients might sit, waiting their turn to place their troubles, difficulties, anxieties before the acutest brain in France, and an inner room wherein that same acute brain—mine, my dear Sir—was wont to ponder and scheme. That apartment was not luxuriously furnished—furniture being very dear in those days—but there were a couple of chairs and a table in the outer office, and a cupboard wherein I kept the frugal repast which served me during the course of a long and laborious day. In the inner office there were more chairs and another table, littered with papers: letters and packets all tied up with pink tape (which cost three sous the metre), and bundles of letters from hundreds of clients, from the highest and the lowest in the land, you understand, people who wrote to me and confided in me to-day as kings and emperors had done in the past. In the antechamber there was a chair-bedstead for Theodore to sleep on when I required him to remain in town, and a chair on which he could sit.

And, of course, there was Theodore!

Ah! my dear Sir, of him I can hardly speak without feeling choked with the magnitude of my emotion. A noble indignation makes me dumb. Theodore, sir, has ever been the cruel thorn that times out of number hath wounded my over-sensitive heart. Think of it! I had picked him out of the gutter! No! no! I do not mean this figuratively! I mean that, actually and in the flesh, I took him up by the collar of his tattered coat and dragged him out of the gutter in the Rue Blanche, where he was grubbing for trifles out of the slime and mud. He was frozen, Sir, and starved—yes, starved! In the intervals of picking filth up out of the mud he held out a hand blue with cold to the passers-by and occasionally picked up a sou. When I found him in that pitiable condition he had exactly twenty centimes between him and absolute starvation.

And I, Sir Hector Ratichon, the confidant of two kings, three autocrats and an emperor, took that man to my bosom—fed him, clothed him, housed him, gave him the post of secretary in my intricate, delicate, immensely important business—and I did this, Sir, at a salary which, in comparison with his twenty centimes, must have seemed a princely one to him.

His duties were light. He was under no obligation to serve me or to be at his post before seven o'clock in the morning, and all that he had to do then was to sweep out the three rooms, fetch water from the well in the courtyard below, light the fire in the iron stove which stood in my inner office, shell the haricots for his own mess of pottage, and put them to boil. During the day his duties were lighter still. He had to run errands for me, open the door to prospective clients, show them into the outer office, explain to them that his master was engaged on affairs relating to the kingdom of France, and generally prove himself efficient, useful and loyal—all of which qualities he assured me, my dear Sir, he possessed to the fullest degree. And I believed him, Sir; I nurtured the scorpion in my over-sensitive bosom! I promised him ten per cent. on all the profits of my business, and all the remnants from my own humble repasts— bread, the skins of luscious sausages, the bones from savoury cutlets, the gravy from the tasty carrots and onions. You would have thought that his gratitude would become boundless, that he would almost worship the benefactor who had poured at his feet the full cornucopia of comfort and luxury. Not so! That man, Sir, was a snake in the grass—a serpent—a crocodile! Even now that I have entirely severed my connexion with that ingrate, I seem to feel the wounds, like dagger-thrusts, which he dealt me with so callous a hand. But I have done with him—done, I tell you! How could I do otherwise than to send him back to the gutter from whence I should never have dragged him? My goodness, he repaid with an ingratitude so black that you, Sir, when you hear the full story of his treachery, will exclaim aghast.

Ah, you shall judge! His perfidy commenced less than a week after I had given him my third best pantaloons and three sous to get his hair cut, thus making a man of him. And yet, you would scarcely believe it, in the matter of the secret documents he behaved toward me like a veritable Judas!

Listen, my dear Sir.

I told you, I believe, that I had my office in the Rue Daunou. You understand that I had to receive my clients—many of whom were of exalted rank—in a fashionable quarter of Paris. But I actually lodged in Passy—being fond of country pursuits and addicted to fresh air—in a humble hostelry under the sign of the "Grey Cat"; and here, too, Theodore had a bed. He would walk to the office a couple of hours before I myself started on the way, and I was wont to arrive as soon after ten o'clock of a morning as I could do conveniently.

On this memorable occasion of which I am about to tell you—it was during the autumn of 1815—I had come to the office unusually early, and had just hung my hat and coat in the outer room, and taken my seat at my desk in the inner office, there to collect my thoughts in preparation for the grave events which the day might bring forth, when, suddenly, an ill-dressed, dour-looking individual entered the room without so much as saying, "By your leave," and after having pushed Theodore—who stood by like a lout—most unceremoniously to one side. Before I had time to recover from my surprise at this unseemly intrusion, the uncouth individual thrust Theodore roughly out of the room, slammed the door in his face, and having satisfied himself that he was alone with, me and that the door was too solid to allow of successful eavesdropping, he dragged the best chair forward—the one, sir, which I reserve for lady visitors.

He threw his leg across it, and, sitting astride, he leaned his elbows over the back and glowered at me as if he meant to frighten me.

"My name is Charles Saurez," he said abruptly, "and I want your assistance in a matter which requires discretion, ingenuity and alertness. Can I have it?"

I was about to make a dignified reply when he literally threw the next words at me: "Name your price, and I will pay it!" he said.

What could I do, save to raise my shoulders in token that the matter of money was one of supreme indifference to me, and my eyebrows in a manner of doubt that M. Charles Saurez had the means wherewith to repay my valuable services? By way of a rejoinder he took out from the inner pocket of his coat a greasy letter-case, and with his exceedingly grimy fingers extracted therefrom some twenty banknotes, which a hasty glance on my part revealed as representing a couple of hundred francs.

"I will give you this as a retaining fee," he said, "if you will undertake the work I want you to do; and I will double the amount when you have carried the work out success fully."

Four hundred francs! It was not lavish, it was perhaps not altogether the price I would have named, but it was vary good, these hard times. You understand? We were all very poor in France in that year 1815 of which I speak.

I am always quite straightforward when I am dealing with a client who means business. I pushed aside the litter of papers in front of me, leaned my elbows upon my desk, rested my chin in my hands, and said briefly:

"M. Charles Saurez, I listen!"

He drew his chair a little closer and dropped his voice almost to a whisper.

"You know the Chancellerie of the Ministry of Foreign Affairs?" he asked.

"Perfectly," I replied.

"You know M. de Marsan's private office? He is chief secretary to M. de Talleyrand."

"No," I said, "but I can find out."

"It is on the first floor, immediately facing the service staircase, and at the end of the long passage which leads to the main staircase."

"Easy to find, then," I remarked.

"Quite. At this hour and until twelve o'clock, M. de Marsan will be occupied in copying a document which I desire to possess. At eleven o'clock precisely there will be a noisy disturbance in the corridor which leads to the main staircase. M. de Marsan, in all probability, will come out of his room to see what the disturbance is about. Will you undertake to be ready at that precise moment to make a dash from the service staircase into the room to seize the document, which no doubt will be lying on the top of the desk, and bring it to an address which I am about to give you?"

"It is risky," I mused.

"Very," he retorted drily, "or I'd do it myself, and not pay you four hundred francs for your trouble."

"Trouble!" I exclaimed, with withering sarcasm.

"Trouble, you call it? If I am caught, it means penal servitude—New Caledonia, perhaps—"

"Exactly," he said, with the same irritating calmness; "and if you succeed it means four hundred francs. Take it or leave it, as you please, but be quick about it. I have no time to waste; it is past nine o'clock already, and if you won't do the work, someone else will."

For a few seconds longer I hesitated. Schemes, both varied and wild, rushed through my active brain: refuse to take this risk, and denounce the plot to the police; refuse it, and run to warn M. de Marsan; refuse it, and— I had little time for reflection. My uncouth client was standing, as it were, with a pistol to my throat—with a pistol and four hundred francs! The police might perhaps give me half a louis for my pains, or they might possibly remember an unpleasant little incident in connexion with the forgery of some Treasury bonds which they have never succeeded in bringing home to me—one never knows! M. de Marsan might throw me a franc, and think himself generous at that!

All things considered, then, when M. Charles Saurez suddenly said, "Well?" with marked impatience, I replied, "Agreed," and within five minutes I had two hundred francs in my pocket, with the prospect of two hundred more during the next four and twenty hours. I was to have a free hand in conducting my own share of the business, and M. Charles Saurez was to call for the document at my lodgings at Passy on the following morning at nine o'clock.

2.

I flatter myself that I conducted the business with remarkable skill. At precisely ten minutes to eleven I rang at the Chancellerie of the Ministry for Foreign Affairs. I was dressed as a respectable commissionnaire, and I carried a letter and a small parcel addressed to M. de Marsan. "First floor," said the concierge curtly, as soon as he had glanced at the superscription on the letter. "Door faces top of the service stairs."

I mounted and took my stand some ten steps below the landing, keeping the door of M. de Marsan's room well in sight. Just as the bells of Notre Dame boomed the hour I heard what sounded like a furious altercation somewhere in the corridor just above me. There was much shouting, then one or two cries of

"Murder!" followed by others of "What is it?" and "What in the name of —— is all this infernal row about?" Doors were opened and banged, there was a general running and rushing along that corridor, and the next minute the door in front of me was opened also, and a young man came out, pen in hand, and shouting just like everybody else:

"What the —— is all this infernal row about?"

"Murder, help!" came from the distant end of the corridor, and M. de Marsan—undoubtedly it was he—did what any other young man under the like circumstances would have done: he ran to see what was happening and to lend a hand in it, if need be. I saw his slim figure disappearing down the corridor at the very moment that I slipped into his room. One glance upon the desk sufficed: there lay the large official-looking document, with the royal signature affixed thereto, and close beside it the copy which M. de Marsan had only half finished—the ink on it was still wet. Hesitation, Sir, would have been fatal. I did not hesitate; not one instant. Three seconds had scarcely elapsed before I picked up the document, together with M. de Marsan's half-finished copy of the same, and a few loose sheets of Chancellerie paper which I thought might be useful. Then I slipped the lot inside my blouse. The bogus letter and parcel I left behind me, and within two minutes of my entry into the room I was descending the service staircase quite unconcernedly, and had gone past the concierge's lodge without being challenged. How thankful I was to breathe once more the pure air of heaven. I had spent an exceedingly agitated five minutes, and even now my anxiety was not altogether at rest. I dared not walk too fast lest I attracted attention, and yet I wanted to put the river, the Pont Neuf, and a half dozen streets between me and the Chancellerie of the Ministry of Foreign Affairs. No one who has not gone through such an exciting adventure as I have just recorded can conceive what were my feelings of relief and of satisfaction when I at last found myself quietly mounting the stairs which led to my office on the top floor of No. 96 Rue Daunou.

3.

Now, I had not said anything to Theodore about this affair. It was certainly arranged between us when he entered my service as confidential clerk and doorkeeper that in lieu of wages, which I could not afford to pay him, he would share my meals with me and have a bed at my expense in the same house at Passy where I lodged; moreover, I would always give him a fair percentage on the profits which I derived from my business. The arrangement suited him very well. I told you that I picked him out of the gutter, and I heard subsequently that he had gone through many an unpleasant skirmish with the police in his day, and if I did not employ him no one else would.

After all, he did earn a more or less honest living by serving me. But in this instance, since I had not even asked for his assistance, I felt that, considering the risks of New Caledonia and a convict ship which I had taken, a paltry four hundred francs could not by any stretch of the imagination rank as a "profit" in a business—and Theodore was not really entitled to a percentage, was he?

So when I returned I crossed the ante-chamber and walked past him with my accustomed dignity; nor did he offer any comment on my get-up. I often affected a disguise in those days, even when I was not engaged in business, and the dress and get-up of a respectable commissionnaire was a favourite one with me. As soon as I had changed I sent him out to make purchases for our luncheon—five sous' worth of stale bread, and ten sous' worth of liver sausage, of which he was inordinately fond. He would take the opportunity on the way of getting moderately drunk on as many glasses of absinthe as he could afford. I saw him go out of the outer door, and then I set to work to examine the precious document.

Well, one glance was sufficient for me to realize its incalculable value! Nothing more or less than a Treaty of Alliance between King Louis XVIII of France and the King of Prussia in connexion with certain schemes of naval construction. I did not understand the whole diplomatic verbiage, but it was pretty clear to my unsophisticated mind that this treaty had been entered into in secret by the two monarchs, and that it was intended to prejudice the interests both of Denmark and of Russia in the Baltic Sea.

I also realized that both the Governments of Denmark and Russia would no doubt pay a very considerable sum for the merest glance at this document, and that my client of this morning was certainly a secret service agent—otherwise a spy—of one of those two countries, who did not choose to take the very severe risks which I had taken this morning, but who would, on the other hand, reap the full reward of the daring coup, whilst I was to be content with four hundred francs!

Now, I am a man of deliberation as well as of action, and at this juncture— feeling that Theodore was still safely out of the way—I thought the whole matter over quietly, and then took what precautions I thought fit for the furthering of my own interests.

To begin with, I set to work to make a copy of the treaty on my own account. I have brought the study of calligraphy to a magnificent degree of perfection, and the writing on the document was easy enough to imitate, as was also the signature of our gracious King Louis and of M. de Talleyrand, who had countersigned it.

If you remember, I had picked up two or three loose sheets of paper off M. de Marsan's desk; these bore the arms of the Chancellerie of Foreign Affairs stamped upon them, and were in every way identical with that on which the original document had been drafted. When I had finished my work I flattered myself that not the greatest calligraphic expert could have detected the slightest difference between the original and the copy which I had made.

The work took me a long time. When at last I folded up the papers and slipped them once more inside my blouse it was close upon two. I wondered why Theodore had not returned with our luncheon, but on going to the little anteroom which divides my office from the outer door, great was my astonishment to see him lolling there on the rickety chair which he affectioned, and half asleep. I had some difficulty in rousing him. Apparently he had got rather drunk while he was out, and had then returned and slept some of his booze off, without thinking that I might be hungry and needing my luncheon.

"Why didn't you let me know you had come back?" I asked curtly, for indeed I was very cross with him.

"I thought you were busy," he replied, with what I thought looked like a leer.

I have never really cared for Theodore, you understand.

However, I partook of our modest luncheon with him in perfect amity and brotherly love, but my mind was busy all the time. I began to wonder if Theodore suspected something; if so, I knew that I could not trust him. He would try and ferret things out, and then demand a share in my hard-earned emoluments to which he was really not entitled. I did not feel safe with that bulky packet of papers on me, and I felt that Theodore's bleary eyes were perpetually fixed upon the bulge in the left-hand side of my coat. At one moment he looked so strange that I thought he meant to knock me down.

So my mind was quickly made up.

After luncheon I would go down to my lodgings at Passy, and I knew of a snug little hiding-place in my room there where the precious documents would be quite safe until such time as I was to hand them—or one of them—to M. Charles Saurez.

This plan I put into execution, and with remarkable ingenuity too.

While Theodore was busy clearing up the debris of our luncheon, I not only gave him the slip, but as I went out I took the precaution of locking the outer door after me, and taking the key away in my pocket. I thus made sure that Theodore could not follow me. I then walked to Passy—a matter of two kilometres—and by four o'clock I had the satisfaction of stowing the papers safely away under one of the tiles in the flooring of my room, and then pulling the strip of carpet in front of my bed snugly over the hiding-place.

Theodore's attic, where he slept, was at the top of the house, whilst my room was on the ground floor, and so I felt that I could now go back quite comfortably to my office in the hope that more remunerative work and more lavish clients would come my way before nightfall.

4.

It was a little after five o'clock when I once more turned the key in the outer door of my rooms in the Rue Daunou.

Theodore did not seem in the least to resent having been locked in for two hours. I think he must have been asleep most of the time. Certainly I heard a good deal of shuffling when first I reached the landing outside the door; but when I actually walked into the apartment with an air of quiet unconcern Theodore was sprawling on the chair-bedstead, with eyes closed, a nose the colour of beetroot, and emitting sounds through his thin, cracked lips which I could not, Sir, describe graphically in your presence.

I took no notice of him, however, even though, as I walked past him, I saw that he opened one bleary eye and watched my every movement. I went straight into my private room and shut the door after me. And here, I assure you, my dear Sir, I literally fell into my favourite chair, overcome with emotion and excitement. Think what I had gone through! The events of the last few hours would have turned any brain less keen, less daring than that of Hector Ratichon. And here was I, alone at last, face to face with the future. What a future, my dear Sir! Fate was smiling on me at last. At last I was destined to reap a rich reward for all the skill, the energy, the devotion, which up to this hour I had placed at the service of my country and my King—or my Emperor, as the case might be—without thought of my own advantage. Here was I now in possession of a document—two documents—each one of which was worth at least a thousand francs to persons whom I could easily approach. One thousand francs! Was I dreaming? Five thousand would certainly be paid by the Government whose agent M. Charles Saurez admittedly was for one glance at that secret treaty which would be so prejudicial to their political interests; whilst M. de Marsan himself would gladly pay another five thousand for the satisfaction of placing the precious document intact before his powerful and irascible uncle.

Ten thousand francs! How few were possessed of such a sum in these days! How much could be done with it! I would not give up business altogether, of course, but with my new capital I would extend it and, there was a certain little house, close to Chantilly, a house with a few acres of kitchen garden and some fruit trees, the possession of which would render me happier than any king. . . . I would marry! Oh, yes! I would certainly marry—found a family. I was still young, my dear Sir, and passably good looking. In fact there was a certain young widow, comely and amiable, who lived not far from Passy, who had on more than one occasion given me to understand that I was more than passably good looking. I had always been susceptible where the fair sex was concerned, and now . . . oh, now! I could pick and choose! The comely widow had a small fortune of her own, and there were others! . . .

Thus I dreamed on for the better part of an hour, until, soon after six o'clock, there was a knock at the outer door and I heard Theodore's shuffling footsteps crossing the small anteroom. There was some muttered conversation, and presently my door was opened and Theodore's ugly face was thrust into the room.

"A lady to see you," he said curtly.

Then, he dropped his voice, smacked his lips, and winked with one eye. "Very pretty," he whispered, "but has a young man with her whom she calls Arthur. Shall I send them in?"

I then and there made up my mind that I would get rid of Theodore now that I could afford to get a proper servant. My business would in future be greatly extended; it would become very important, and I was beginning to detest

Theodore. But I said "Show the lady in!" with becoming dignity, and a few moments later a beautiful woman entered my room.

I was vaguely conscious that a creature of my own sex walked in behind her, but of him I took no notice. I rose to greet the lady and invited her to sit down, but I had the annoyance of seeing the personage whom deliberately she called "Arthur" coming familiarly forward and leaning over the back of her chair.

I hated him. He was short and stout and florid, with an impertinent-looking moustache, and hair that was very smooth and oily save for two tight curls, which looked like the horns of a young goat, on each side of the centre parting. I hated him cordially, and had to control my feelings not to show him the contempt which I felt for his fatuousness and his air of self-complacency. Fortunately the beautiful being was the first to address me, and thus I was able to ignore the very presence of the detestable man.

"You are M. Ratichon, I believe," she said in a voice that was dulcet and adorably tremulous, like the voice of some sweet, shy young thing in the presence of genius and power.

"Hector Ratichon," I replied calmly. "Entirely at your service, Mademoiselle." Then I added, with gentle, encouraging kindliness, "Mademoiselle . . . ?"

"My name is Geoffroy," she replied, "Madeleine Geoffroy."

She raised her eyes—such eyes, my dear Sir!—of a tender, luscious grey, fringed with lashes and dewy with tears. I met her glance. Something in my own eyes must have spoken with mute eloquence of my distress, for she went on quickly and with a sweet smile. "And this," she said, pointing to her companion, "is my brother, Arthur Geoffroy."

An exclamation of joyful surprise broke from my lips, and I beamed and smiled on M. Arthur, begged him to be seated, which he refused, and finally I myself sat down behind my desk. I now looked with unmixed benevolence on both my clients, and then perceived that the lady's exquisite face bore unmistakable signs of recent sorrow.

"And now, Mademoiselle," I said, as soon as I had taken up a position indicative of attention and of encouragement, "will you deign to tell me how I can have the honour to serve you?"

"Monsieur," she began in a voice that trembled with emotion, "I have come to you in the midst of the greatest distress that any human being has ever been called upon to bear. It was by the merest accident that I heard of you. I have been to the police; they cannot—will not—act without I furnish them with certain information which it is not in my power to give them. Then when I was half distraught with despair, a kindly agent there spoke to me of you. He said that you were attached to the police as a voluntary agent, and that they sometimes put work in your way which did not happen to be within their own scope. He also said that sometimes you were successful."

"Nearly always, Mademoiselle," I broke in firmly and with much dignity. "Once more I beg of you to tell me in what way I may have the honour to serve you."

"It is not for herself, Monsieur," here interposed M. Arthur, whilst a blush suffused Mlle. Geoffroy's lovely face, "that my sister desires to consult you, but for her fiancé M. de Marsan, who is very ill indeed, hovering, in fact, between life and death. He could not come in person. The matter is one that demands the most profound secrecy."

"You may rely on my discretion, Monsieur," I murmured, without showing, I flatter myself, the slightest trace of that astonishment which, at mention of M. de Marsan's name, had nearly rendered me speechless.

"M. de Marsan came to see me in utmost distress, Monsieur," resumed the lovely creature. "He had no one in whom he could—or rather dared—confide. He is in the Chancellerie for Foreign Affairs. His uncle M. de Talleyrand thinks a great deal of him and often entrusts him with very delicate work. This morning he gave M. de Marsan a valuable paper to copy—a paper, Monsieur, the importance of which it were impossible to overestimate. The very safety of this country, the honour of our King, are involved in it. I cannot tell you its exact contents, and it is because I would not tell more about it to the police that they would not help me in any way, and referred me to you. How could they, said the chief Commissary to me, run after a document the contents of which they did not even know? But you will be satisfied with what I have told you, will you not, my dear M. Ratichon?" she continued, with a pathetic quiver in her voice and a look of appeal in her eyes which St. Anthony himself could not have resisted, "and help me to regain possession of that paper, the final loss of which would cost M. de Marsan his life."

To say that my feeling of elation of a while ago had turned to one of supreme beatitude would be to put it very mildly indeed. To think that here was this lovely being in tears before me, and that it lay in my power to dry those tears with a word and to bring a smile round those perfect lips, literally made my mouth water in anticipation—for I am sure that you will have guessed, just as I did in a moment, that the valuable document of which this adorable being was speaking, was snugly hidden away under the flooring of my room in Passy. I hated that unknown de Marsan. I hated this Arthur who leaned so familiarly over her chair, but I had the power to render her a service beside which their lesser claims on her regard would pale.

However, I am not the man to act on impulse, even at a moment like this. I wanted to think the whole matter over first, and . . . well . . . I had made up my mind to demand five thousand francs when I handed the document over to my first client to-morrow morning. At any rate, for the moment I acted—if I may say so—with great circumspection and dignity.

"I must presume, Mademoiselle," I said in my most business-like manner, "that the document you speak of has been stolen."

"Stolen, Monsieur," she assented whilst the tears once more gathered in her eyes, "and M. de Marsan now lies at death's door with a terrible attack of brain fever, brought on by shock when he discovered the loss."

"How and when was it stolen?" I asked.

"Some time during the morning," she replied. "M. de Talleyrand gave the document to M. de Marsan at nine o'clock, telling him that he wanted the copy by midday. M. de Marsan set to work at once, laboured uninterruptedly until about eleven o'clock, when a loud altercation, followed by cries of 'Murder!' and of 'Help!' and proceeding from the corridor outside his door, caused him to run out of the room in order to see what was happening. The altercation turned out to be between two men who had pushed their way into the building by the main staircase, and who became very abusive to the gendarme who ordered them out. The men were not hurt; nevertheless they screamed as if they were being murdered. They took to their heels quickly enough, and I don't know what has become of them, but . . ."

"But," I concluded blandly, "whilst M. de Marsan was out of the room the precious document was stolen."

"It was, Monsieur," exclaimed Mlle. Geoffroy piteously. "You will find it for us . . . will you not?"

Then she added more calmly: "My brother and I are offering ten thousand francs reward for the recovery of the document."

I did not fall off my chair, but I closed my eyes. The vision which the lovely lady's words had conjured up dazzled me.

"Mademoiselle," I said with solemn dignity, "I pledge you my word of honour that I will find the document for you and lay it at your feet or die in your service. Give me twenty hours, during which I will move heaven and earth to discover the thief. I will go at once to the Chancellerie and collect what evidence I can. I have worked under M. de Robespierre, Mademoiselle, under the great Napoléon, and under the illustrious Fouché! I have never been known to fail, once I have set my mind upon a task."

"In that case you will earn your ten thousand francs, my friend," said the odious Arthur drily, "and my sister and M. de Marsan will still be your debtors. Are there any questions you would like to ask before we go?"

"None," I said loftily, choosing to ignore his sneering manner. "If Mademoiselle deigns to present herself here to-morrow at two o'clock I will have news to communicate to her."

You will admit that I carried off the situation in a becoming manner. Both Mademoiselle and Arthur Geoffroy gave me a few more details in connexion with the affair. To these details I listened with well simulated interest. Of course, they did not know that there were no details in connexion with this affair that I did not know already. My heart was actually dancing within my bosom. The future was so entrancing that the present appeared like a dream; the lovely being before me seemed like an angel, an emissary from above come to tell me of the happiness which was in store for me. The house near Chantilly—the little widow—the kitchen garden—the magic words went on hammering in my brain. I longed now to be rid of my visitors, to be alone once more, so as to think out the epilogue of this glorious adventure. Ten thousand francs was the reward offered me by this adorable creature! Well, then, why should not M. Charles

Saurez, on his side, pay me another ten thousand for the same document, which was absolutely undistinguishable from the first?

Ten thousand, instead of two hundred which he had the audacity to offer me!

Seven o'clock had struck before I finally bowed my clients out of the room. Theodore had gone. The lazy lout would never stay as much as five minutes after his appointed time, so I had to show the adorable creature and her fat brother out of the premises myself. But I did not mind that. I flatter myself that I can always carry off an awkward situation in a dignified manner. A brief allusion to the inefficiency of present-day servants, a jocose comment on my own simplicity of habits, and the deed was done. M. Arthur Geoffroy and Mademoiselle Madeleine his sister were half-way down the stairs. A quarter of an hour later I was once more out in the streets of Paris. It was a beautiful, balmy night. I had two hundred francs in my pocket and there was a magnificent prospect of twenty thousand francs before me! I could afford some slight extravagance. I had dinner at one of the fashionable restaurants on the quay, and I remained some time out on the terrace sipping my coffee and liqueur, dreaming dreams such as I had never dreamed before. At ten o'clock I was once more on my way to Passy.

5.

When I turned the corner of the street and came is sight of the squalid house where I lodged, I felt like a being from another world. Twenty thousand francs—a fortune!—was waiting for me inside those dingy walls. Yes, twenty thousand, for by now I had fully made up my mind. I had two documents concealed beneath the floor of my bedroom—one so like the other that none could tell them apart. One of these I would restore to the lovely being who had offered me ten thousand francs for it, and the other I would sell to my first and uncouth client for another ten thousand francs!

Four hundred! Bah! Ten thousand shall you pay for the treaty, my friend of the Danish or Russian Secret Service! Ten thousand!—it is worth that to you!

In that happy frame of mind I reached the front door of my dingy abode. Imagine my surprise on being confronted with two agents of police, each with fixed bayonet, who refused to let me pass.

"But I lodge here," I said.

"Your name?" queried one of the men. "Hector Ratichon," I replied. Whereupon they gave me leave to enter.

It was very mysterious. My heart beat furiously. Fear for the safety of my precious papers held me in a death-like grip. I ran straight to my room, locked the door after me, and pulled the curtains together in front of the window. Then, with hands that trembled as if with ague, I pulled aside the strip of carpet which concealed the hiding-place of what meant a fortune to me.

I nearly fainted with joy; the papers were there—quite safely. I took them out and replaced them inside my coat.

Then I ran up to see if Theodore was in. I found him in bed. He told me that he had left the office whilst my visitors were still with me, as he felt terribly sick. He had been greatly upset when, about an hour ago, the maid-of-all-work had informed him that the police were in the house, that they would allow no one—except the persons lodging in the house—to enter it, and no one, once in, would be allowed to leave. How long these orders would hold good Theodore did not know.

I left him moaning and groaning and declaring that he felt very ill, and I went in quest of information. The corporal in command of the gendarmes was exceedingly curt with me at first, but after a time he unbent and condescended to tell me that my landlord had been denounced for permitting a Bonapartiste club to hold its sittings in his house. So far so good. Such denunciations were very frequent these days, and often ended unpleasantly for those concerned, but the affair had obviously nothing to do with me. I felt that I could breathe again. But there was still the matter of the consigne. If no one, save the persons who lodged in the house, would be allowed to enter it, how would M. Charles Saurez contrive to call for the stolen document and, incidentally, to hand me over the ten thousand francs I was hoping for? And if no one, once inside the house, would be allowed to leave it, how could I meet Mlle. Geoffroy to-morrow at two o'clock in my office and receive ten thousand francs from her in exchange for the precious paper?

Moreover the longer the police stayed in this house and poked their noses about in affairs that concerned hardworking citizens like myself—why—the greater the risk would be of the matter of the stolen document coming to light.

It was positively maddening.

I never undressed that night, but just lay down on my bed, thinking. The house was very still at times, but at others I could hear the tramp of the police agents up and down the stairs and also outside my window. The latter gave on a small, dilapidated back garden which had a wooden fence at the end of it. Beyond it were some market gardens belonging to a M. Lorraine. It did not take me very long to realize that that way lay my fortune of twenty thousand francs. But for the moment I remained very still. My plan was already made. At about midnight I went to the window and opened it cautiously. I had heard no noise from that direction for some time, and I bent my ear to listen.

Not a sound! Either the sentry was asleep, or he had gone on his round, and for a few moments the way was free. Without a moment's hesitation I swung my leg over the sill.

Still no sound. My heart beat so fast that I could almost hear it. The night was very dark. A thin mist-like drizzle was falling; in fact the weather conditions were absolutely perfect for my purpose. With utmost wariness I allowed myself to drop from the window-ledge on to the soft ground below.

If I was caught by the sentry I had my answer ready: I was going to meet my sweetheart at the end of the garden. It is an excuse which always meets with the sympathy of every true-hearted Frenchman. The sentry would, of course, order me back to my room, but I doubt if he would ill-use me; the denunciation was against the landlord, not against me.

Still not a sound. I could have danced with joy. Five minutes more and I would be across the garden and over that wooden fence, and once more on my way to fortune. My fall from the window had been light, as my room was on the ground floor; but I had fallen on my knees, and now, as I picked myself up, I looked up, and it seemed to me as if I saw Theodore's ugly face at his attic window. Certainly there was a light there, and I may have been mistaken as to Theodore's face being visible. The very next second the light was extinguished and I was left in doubt.

But I did not pause to think. In a moment I was across the garden, my hands gripped the top of the wooden fence, I hoisted myself up—with some difficulty, I confess—but at last I succeeded. I threw my leg over and gently dropped down on the other side.

Then suddenly two rough arms encircled my waist, and before I could attempt to free myself a cloth was thrown over my head, and I was lifted up and carried away, half suffocated and like an insentient bundle.

When the cloth was removed from my face I was half sitting, half lying, in an arm-chair in a strange room which was lighted by an oil lamp that hung from the ceiling above. In front of me stood M. Arthur Geoffroy and that beast Theodore.

M. Arthur Geoffroy was coolly folding up the two valuable papers for the possession of which I had risked a convict ship and New Caledonia, and which would have meant affluence for me for many days to come.

It was Theodore who had removed the cloth from my face. As soon as I had recovered my breath I made a rush for him, for I wanted to strangle him. But M. Arthur Geoffroy was too quick and too strong for me. He pushed me back into the chair.

"Easy, easy, M. Ratichon," he said pleasantly; "do not vent your wrath upon this good fellow. Believe me, though his actions may have deprived you of a few thousand francs, they have also saved you from lasting and biting remorse. This document, which you stole from M. de Marsan and so ingeniously duplicated, involved the honour of our King and our country, as well as the life of an innocent man. My sister's fiancé would never have survived the loss of the document which had been entrusted to his honour."

"I would have returned it to Mademoiselle to-morrow," I murmured.

"Only one copy of it, I think," he retorted; "the other you would have sold to whichever spy of the Danish or Russian Governments happened to have employed you in this discreditable business."

"How did you know?" I said involuntarily.

"Through a very simple process of reasoning, my good M. Ratichon," he replied blandly. "You are a very clever man, no doubt, but the cleverest of us is at times apt to make a mistake. You made two, and I profited by them. Firstly, after my sister and I left you this afternoon, you never made the slightest pretence of making inquiries or collecting information about the mysterious theft of the document. I kept an eye on you throughout the evening. You left your office and strolled for a while on the quays; you had an excellent dinner at the Restaurant des Anglais; then you settled down to your coffee and liqueur. Well, my good M. Ratichon, obviously you would have been more active in the matter if you had not known exactly where and when and how to lay your hands upon the document, for the recovery of which my sister had offered you ten thousand francs."

I groaned. I had not been quite so circumspect as I ought to have been, but who would have thought—

"I have had something to do with police work in my day," continued M. Geoffroy blandly, "though not of late years; but my knowledge of their methods is not altogether rusty and my powers of observation are not yet dulled. During my sister's visit to you this afternoon I noticed the blouse and cap of a commissionnaire lying in a bundle in a corner of your room. Now, though M. de Marsan has been in a burning fever since he discovered his loss, he kept just sufficient presence of mind at the moment to say nothing about that loss to any of the Chancellerie officials, but to go straight home to his apartments in the Rue Royale and to send for my sister and for me. When we came to him he was already partly delirious, but he pointed to a parcel and a letter which he had brought away from his office. The parcel proved to be an empty box and the letter a blank sheet of paper; but the most casual inquiry of the concierge at the Chancellerie elicited the fact that a commissionaire had brought these things in the course of the morning. That was your second mistake, my good M. Ratichon; not a very grave one, perhaps, but I have been in the police, and somehow, the moment I caught sight of that blouse and cap in your office, I could not help connecting it with the commissionnaire who had brought a bogus parcel and letter to my future brother-in-law a few minutes before that mysterious and unexplained altercation took place in the corridor."

Again I groaned. I felt as a child in the hands of that horrid creature who seemed to be dissecting all the thoughts which had run riot through my mind these past twenty hours.

"It was all very simple, my good M. Ratichon," now concluded my tormentor still quite amiably. "Another time you will have to be more careful, will you not? You will also have to bestow more confidence upon your partner or servant. Directly I had seen that commissionnaire's blouse and cap, I set to work to make friends with M. Theodore. When my sister and I left your office in the Rue Daunou, we found him waiting for us at the bottom of the stairs. Five francs loosened his tongue: he suspected that you were up to some game in which you did not mean him to have a share; he also told us that you had spent two hours in laborious writing, and that you and he both lodged at a dilapidated little inn, called the 'Grey Cat,' in Passy. I think he was rather disappointed that we did not shower more questions, and therefore more emoluments, upon him. Well, after I had denounced this house to the police as a Bonapartiste club, and saw it put under the usual consigne, I bribed the corporal of the gendarmerie in charge of it to let me have Theodore's company for the little job I had in hand, and also to clear the back garden of sentries so as to give you a chance and the desire to escape. All the rest you know. Money will do many things, my good M. Ratichon, and you see how simple it all was. It would have been still more simple if the stolen document had not been such an important one that the very existence of it must be kept a secret even from the police. So I could not have you shadowed and arrested as a thief in the usual manner! However, I have the document and its ingenious copy, which is all that matters. Would to God," he added with a suppressed curse, "that I could get hold equally easily of the Secret Service agent to whom you, a Frenchman, were going to sell the honour of your country!"

Then it was that—though broken in spirit and burning with thoughts of the punishment I would mete out to Theodore—my full faculties returned to me, and I queried abruptly:

"What would you give to get him?"

"Five hundred francs," he replied without hesitation. "Can you find him?"

"Make it a thousand," I retorted, "and you shall have him."

"How?"

"Will you give me five hundred francs now," I insisted, "and another five hundred when you have the man, and I will tell you?"

"Agreed," he said impatiently.

But I was not to be played with by him again. I waited in silence until he had taken a pocket-book from the inside of his coat and counted out five hundred francs, which he kept in his hand.

"Now—" he commanded.

"The man," I then announced calmly, "will call on me for the document at my lodgings at the hostelry of the 'Grey Cat' to-morrow morning at nine o'clock."

"Good," rejoined M. Geoffroy. "We shall be there."

He made no demur about giving me the five hundred francs, but half my pleasure in receiving them vanished when I saw Theodore's bleary eyes fixed ravenously upon them.

"Another five hundred francs," M. Geoffroy went on quietly, "will be yours as soon as the spy is in our hands."

I did get that further five hundred of course, for M. Charles Saurez was punctual to the minute, and M. Geoffroy was there with the police to apprehend him. But to think that I might have had twenty thousand—!

And I had to give Theodore fifty francs on the transaction, as he threatened me with the police when I talked of giving him the sack.

But we were quite good friends again after that until— But you shall judge.

CHAPTER II

A FOOL'S PARADISE

1.

Ah! my dear Sir, I cannot tell you how poor we all were in France in that year of grace 1816—so poor, indeed, that a dish of roast pork was looked upon as a feast, and a new gown for the wife an unheard-of luxury.

The war had ruined everyone. Twenty-two years! and hopeless humiliation and defeat at the end of it. The Emperor handed over to the English; a Bourbon sitting on the throne of France; crowds of foreign soldiers still lording it all over the country—until the country had paid its debts to her foreign invaders, and thousands of our own men still straggling home through Germany and Belgium—the remnants of Napoléon's Grand Army—ex-prisoners of war, or scattered units who had found their weary way home at last, shoeless, coatless, half starved and perished from cold and privations, unfit for housework, for agriculture, or for industry, fit only to follow their fallen hero, as they had done through a quarter of a century, to victory and to death.

With me, Sir, business in Paris was almost at a standstill. I, who had been the confidential agent of two kings, three democrats and one emperor; I, who had held diplomatic threads in my hands which had caused thrones to totter and tyrants to quake, and who had brought more criminals and intriguers to book than any other man alive—I now sat in my office in the Rue Daunou day after day with never a client to darken my doors, even whilst crime and political intrigue were more rife in Paris than they had been in the most corrupt days of the Revolution and the Consulate.

I told you, I think, that I had forgiven Theodore his abominable treachery in connexion with the secret naval treaty, and we were the best of friends—that is, outwardly, of course. Within my inmost heart I felt, Sir, that I could never again trust that shameless traitor—that I had in very truth nurtured a serpent in my bosom. But I am proverbially tender-hearted. You will believe me or not, I simply could not turn that vermin out into the street. He deserved it! Oh, even he would have admitted when he was quite sober, which was not often, that I had every right to give him the sack, to send him back to the gutter whence he had come, there to grub once more for scraps of filth and to stretch a half-frozen hand to the charity of the passers by.

But I did not do it, Sir. No, I did not do it. I kept him on at the office as my confidential servant; I gave him all the crumbs that fell from mine own table, and he helped himself to the rest. I made as little difference as I could in my intercourse with him. I continued to treat him almost as an equal. The only difference I did make in our mode of life was that I no longer gave him bed and board at the hostelry where I lodged in Passy, but placed the chair-bedstead in the anteroom of the office permanently at his disposal, and allowed him five sous a day for his breakfast.

But owing to the scarcity of business that now came my way, Theodore had little or nothing to do, and he was in very truth eating his head off, and with that, grumble, grumble all the time, threatening to leave me, if you please, to leave my service for more remunerative occupation. As if anyone else would dream of employing such an out-at-elbows mudlark—a jail-bird, Sir, if you'll believe me.

Thus the Spring of 1816 came along. Spring, Sir, with its beauty and its promises, and the thoughts of love which come eternally in the minds of those who have not yet wholly done with youth. Love, Sir! I dreamed of it on those long, weary afternoons in April, after I had consumed my scanty repast, and whilst Theodore in the anteroom was snoring like a hog. At even, when tired out and thirsty, I would sit for a while outside a humble café on the outer boulevards, I watched the amorous couples wander past me on their way to happiness. At night I could not sleep, and bitter were my thoughts, my revilings against a cruel fate that had condemned me—a man with so sensitive a heart and so generous a nature—to the sorrows of perpetual solitude.

That, Sir, was my mood, when on a never-to-be-forgotten afternoon toward the end of April, I sat mooning disconsolately in my private room and a timid rat-tat at the outer door of the apartment roused Theodore from his brutish slumbers. I heard him shuffling up to the door, and I hurriedly put my necktie straight and smoothed my hair, which had become disordered despite the fact that I had only indulged in a very abstemious déjeuner.

When I said that the knock at my door was in the nature of a timid rat-rat I did not perhaps describe it quite accurately. It was timid, if you will understand me, and yet bold, as coming from one who might hesitate to enter and nevertheless feels assured of welcome. Obviously a client, I thought.

Effectively, Sir, the next moment my eyes were gladdened by the sight of a lovely woman, beautifully dressed, young, charming, smiling but to hide her anxiety, trustful, and certainly wealthy.

The moment she stepped into the room I knew that she was wealthy; there was an air of assurance about her which only those are able to assume who are not pestered with creditors. She wore two beautiful diamond rings upon her hands outside her perfectly fitting glove, and her bonnet was adorned with flowers so exquisitely fashioned that a butterfly would have been deceived and would have perched on it with delight.

Her shoes were of the finest kid, shiny at the toes like tiny mirrors, whilst her dainty ankles were framed in the filmy lace frills of her pantalets.

Within the wide brim of her bonnet her exquisite face appeared like a rosebud nestling in a basket. She smiled when I rose to greet her, gave me a look that sent my susceptible heart a-flutter and caused me to wish that I had not taken that bottle-green coat of mine to the Mont de Piété only last week. I offered her a seat, which she took, arranging her skirts about her with inimitable grace.

"One moment," I added, as soon as she was seated, "and I am entirely at your service."

I took up pen and paper—an unfinished letter which I always keep handy for the purpose—and wrote rapidly. It always looks well for a lawyer or an *agent confidentiel* to keep a client waiting for a moment or two while he attends to the enormous pressure of correspondence which, if allowed to accumulate for five minutes, would immediately overwhelm him. I signed and folded the letter, threw it with a nonchalant air into a basket filled to the brim with others of equal importance, buried my face in my hands for a few seconds as if to collect my thoughts, and finally said:

"And now, Mademoiselle, will you deign to tell me what procures me the honour of your visit?"

The lovely creature had watched my movements with obvious impatience, a frown upon her exquisite brow. But now she plunged straightway into her story.

"Monsieur," she said with that pretty, determined air which became her so well, "my name is Estelle Bachelier. I am an orphan, an heiress, and have need of help and advice. I did not know to whom to apply. Until three months ago I was poor and had to earn my living by working in a milliner's shop in the Rue St. Honoré. The concierge in the house where I used to lodge is my only friend, but she cannot help me for reasons which will presently be made clear to you. She told me, however, that she had a nephew named Theodore, who was clerk to M. Ratichon, advocate and confidential agent. She gave me your address; and as I knew no one else I determined to come and consult you."

I flatter myself, that though my countenance is exceptionally mobile, I possess marvellous powers for keeping it impassive when necessity arises. In this instance, at mention of Theodore's name, I showed neither surprise nor indignation. Yet you will readily understand that I felt both. Here was that man, once more revealed as a traitor. Theodore had an aunt of whom he had never as much as breathed a word. He had an aunt, and that aunt a concierge—*ipso facto*, if I may so express it, a woman of some substance, who, no doubt, would often have been only too pleased to extend hospitality to the man who had so signally befriended her nephew; a woman, Sir, who was undoubtedly possessed of savings which both reason and gratitude would cause her to invest in an old-established and substantial business run by a trustworthy and capable man, such, for instance, as the bureau of a confidential agent in a good quarter of Paris, which, with the help of a little capital, could be rendered highly lucrative and beneficial to all those, concerned.

I determined then and there to give Theodore a piece of my mind and to insist upon an introduction to his aunt. After which I begged the beautiful creature to proceed.

"My father, Monsieur," she continued, "died three months ago, in England, whither he had emigrated when I was a mere child, leaving my poor mother to struggle along for a livelihood as best she could. My mother died last year, Monsieur, and I have hard a hard life; and now it seems that my father made a fortune in England and left it all to me."

I was greatly interested in her story.

"The first intimation I had of it, Monsieur, was three months ago, when I had a letter from an English lawyer in London telling me that my father, Jean Paul Bachelier—that was his name, Monsieur—had died out there and made a will leaving all his money, about one hundred thousand francs, to me."

"Yes, yes!" I murmured, for my throat felt parched and my eyes dim.

Hundred thousand francs! Ye gods!

"It seems," she proceeded demurely, "that my father put it in his will that the English lawyers were to pay me the interest on the money until I married or reached the age of twenty-one. Then the whole of the money was to be handed over to me."

I had to steady myself against the table or I would have fallen over backwards! This godlike creature, to whom the sum of one hundred thousand francs was to be paid over when she married, had come to me for help and advice! The thought sent my brain reeling! I am so imaginative!

"Proceed, Mademoiselle, I pray you," I contrived to say with dignified calm.

"Well, Monsieur, as I don't know a word of English, I took the letter to Mr. Farewell, who is the English traveller for Madame Cécile, the milliner for whom I worked. He is a kind, affable gentleman and was most helpful to me. He was, as a matter of fact, just going over to England the very next day. He offered to go and see the English lawyers for me, and to bring me back all particulars of my dear father's death and of my unexpected fortune."

"And," said I, for she had paused a moment, "did Mr. Farewell go to England on your behalf?"

"Yes, Monsieur. He went and returned about a fortnight later. He had seen the English lawyers, who confirmed all the good news which was contained in their letter. They took, it seems, a great fancy to Mr. Farewell, and told him that since I was obviously too young to live alone and needed a guardian to look after my interests, they would appoint him my guardian, and suggested that I should make my home with him until I was married or had attained the age of twenty-one. Mr. Farewell told me that though this arrangement might be somewhat inconvenient in his bachelor establishment, he had been unable to resist the entreaties of the English lawyers, who felt that no one was more fitted for such onerous duties than himself, seeing that he was English and so obviously my friend."

"The scoundrel! The blackguard!" I exclaimed in an unguarded outburst of fury. . . .

"Your pardon, Mademoiselle," I added more calmly, seeing that the lovely creature was gazing at me with eyes full of astonishment not unmixed with distrust, "I am anticipating. Am I to understand, then, that you have made your home with this Mr. Farewell?"

"Yes, Monsieur, at number sixty-five Rue des Pyramides."

"Is he a married man?" I asked casually.

"He is a widower, Monsieur."

"Middle-aged?"

"Quite elderly, Monsieur."

I could have screamed with joy. I was not yet forty myself.

"Why!" she added gaily, "he is thinking of retiring from business—he is, as I said, a commercial traveller—in favour of his nephew, M. Adrien Cazalès."

Once more I had to steady myself against the table. The room swam round me. One hundred thousand francs!—a lovely creature!—an unscrupulous widower!—an equally dangerous young nephew. I rose and tottered to the window. I flung it wide open—a thing I never do save at moments of acute crises.

The breath of fresh air did me good. I returned to my desk, and was able once more to assume my habitual dignity and presence of mind.

"In all this, Mademoiselle," I said in my best professional manner, "I do not gather how I can be of service to you."

"I am coming to that, Monsieur," she resumed after a slight moment of hesitation, even as an exquisite blush suffused her damask cheeks. "You must know that at first I was very happy in the house of my new guardian. He was exceedingly kind to me, though there were times already when I fancied . . ."

She hesitated—more markedly this time—and the blush became deeper on her cheeks. I groaned aloud.

"Surely he is too old," I suggested.

"Much too old," she assented emphatically.

Once more I would have screamed with joy had not a sharp pang, like a dagger-thrust, shot through my heart.

"But the nephew, eh?" I said as jocosely, as indifferently as I could. "Young M. Cazalès? What?"

"Oh!" she replied with perfect indifference. "I hardly ever see him."

Unfortunately it were not seemly for an avocat and the *agent confidentiel* of half the Courts of Europe to execute the measures of a polka in the presence of a client, or I would indeed have jumped up and danced with glee. The happy thoughts were hammering away in my mind: "The old one is much too old—the young one she never sees!" and I could have knelt down and kissed the hem of her gown for the exquisite indifference with which she had uttered those magic words: "Oh! I hardly ever see him!"—words which converted my brightest hopes into glowing possibilities.

But, as it was, I held my emotions marvellously in check, and with perfect sang-froid once more asked the beauteous creature how I could be of service to her in her need.

"Of late, Monsieur," she said, as she raised a pair of limpid, candid blue eyes to mine, "my position in Mr. Farewell's house has become intolerable. He pursues me with his attentions, and he has become insanely jealous. He will not allow me to speak to anyone, and has even forbidden M. Cazalès, his own nephew, the house. Not that I care about that," she added with an expressive shrug of the shoulders.

"He has forbidden M. Cazalès the house," rang like a paean in my ear. "Not that she cares about that! Tra la, la, la, la, la!" What I actually contrived to say with a measured and judicial air was:

"If you deign to entrust me with the conduct of your affairs, I would at once communicate with the English lawyers in your name and suggest to them the advisability of appointing another guardian. . . . I would suggest, for instance . . . er . . . that I . . ."

"How can you do that, Monsieur?" she broke in somewhat impatiently, "seeing that I cannot possibly tell you who these lawyers are?"

"Eh?" I queried, gasping.

"I neither know their names nor their residence in England."

Once more I gasped. "Will you explain?" I murmured.

"It seems, Monsieur, that while my dear mother lived she always refused to take a single sou from my father, who had so basely deserted her. Of course, she did not know that he was making a fortune over in England, nor that he was making diligent inquiries as to her whereabouts when he felt that he was going to die. Thus, he discovered that she had died the previous year and that I was working in the atelier of Madame Cécile, the well-known milliner. When the English lawyers wrote to me at that address they, of course, said that they would require all my papers of identification before they paid any money over to me, and so, when Mr. Farewell went over to England, he took all my papers with him and . . ."

She burst into tears and exclaimed piteously:

"Oh! I have nothing now, Monsieur—nothing to prove who I am! Mr. Farewell took everything, even the original letter which the English lawyers wrote to me."

"Farewell," I urged, "can be forced by the law to give all your papers up to you."

"Oh! I have nothing now, Monsieur—he threatened to destroy all my papers unless I promised to become his wife! And I haven't the least idea how and where to find the English lawyers. I don't remember either their name or their address; and if I did, how could I prove my identity to their satisfaction? I don't know a soul in Paris save a few irresponsible millinery apprentices and Madame Cécile, who, no doubt, is hand in glove with Mr. Farewell. I am all alone in the world and friendless. . . . I have come to you, Monsieur, in my distress . . . and you will help me, will you not?"

She looked more adorable in grief than she had ever done before.

To tell you that at this moment visions floated in my mind, before which Dante's visions of Paradise would seem pale and tame, were but to put it mildly. I was literally soaring in heaven. For you see I am a man of intellect and of action. No sooner do I see possibilities before me than my brain soars in an empyrean whilst conceiving daring plans for my body's permanent abode in elysium. At this present moment, for instance—to name but a few of the beatific visions which literally dazzled me with their radiance—I could see my fair client as a lovely and blushing bride by my side, even whilst Messieurs X. and X., the two still unknown English lawyers, handed me a heavy bag which bore the legend "One hundred thousand francs." I could see . . . But I had not the time now to dwell on these ravishing dreams. The beauteous creature was waiting for my decision. She had placed her fate in my hands; I placed my hand on my heart.

"Mademoiselle," I said solemnly, "I will be your adviser and your friend. Give me but a few days' grace, every hour, every minute of which I will spend in your service. At the end of that time I will not only have learned the name and address of the English lawyers, but I will have communicated with them on your behalf, and all your papers proving your identity will be in your hands. Then we can come to a decision with regard to a happier and more comfortable home for you. In the meanwhile I entreat you to do nothing that may precipitate Mr. Farewell's actions. Do not encourage his advances, but do not repulse them, and above all keep me well informed of everything that goes on in his house."

She spoke a few words of touching gratitude, then she rose, and with a gesture of exquisite grace she extracted a hundred-franc note from her reticule and placed it upon my desk.

"Mademoiselle," I protested with splendid dignity, "I have done nothing as yet."

"Ah! but you will, Monsieur," she entreated in accents that completed my subjugation to her charms. "Besides, you do not know me! How could I expect you to work for me and not to know if, in the end, I should repay you for all your trouble? I pray you to take this small sum without demur. Mr. Farewell keeps me well supplied with pocket money. There will be another hundred for you when you place the papers in my hands."

I bowed to her, and, having once more assured her of my unswerving loyalty to her interests, I accompanied her to the door, and anon saw her graceful figure slowly descend the stairs and then disappear along the corridor.

Then I went back to my room, and was only just in time to catch Theodore calmly pocketing the hundred-franc note which my fair client had left on the table. I secured the note and I didn't give him a black eye, for it was no use putting him in a bad temper when there was so much to do.

2.

That very same evening I interviewed the concierge at No. 65 Rue des Pyramides. From him I learned that Mr. Farewell lived on a very small income on the top floor of the house, that his household consisted of a housekeeper who cooked and did the work of the apartment for him, and an odd-job man who came every morning to clean boots, knives, draw water and carry up fuel from below. I also learned that there was a good deal of gossip in the house anent the presence in Mr. Farewell's bachelor establishment of a young and beautiful girl, whom he tried to keep a virtual prisoner under his eye.

The next morning, dressed in a shabby blouse, alpaca cap, and trousers frayed out round the ankles, I—Hector Ratichon, the confidant of kings—was lounging under the porte-cochere of No. 65 Rue des Pyramides. I was watching the movements of a man, similarly attired to myself, as he crossed and recrossed the courtyard to draw water from the well or to fetch wood from one of the sheds, and then disappeared up the main staircase.

A casual, tactful inquiry of the concierge assured me that that man was indeed in the employ of Mr. Farewell.

I waited as patiently and inconspicuously as I could, and at ten o'clock I saw that my man had obviously finished his work for the morning and had finally come down the stairs ready to go home. I followed him.

I will not speak of the long halt in the cabaret du Chien Noir, where he spent an hour and a half in the company of his friends, playing dominoes and drinking eau-de-vie whilst I had perforce to cool my heels outside. Suffice it to say that I did follow him to his house just behind the fish-market, and that half an hour later, tired out but triumphant, having knocked at his door, I was admitted into the squalid room which he occupied.

He surveyed me with obvious mistrust, but I soon reassured him.

"My friend Mr. Farewell has recommended you to me," I said with my usual affability. "I was telling him just awhile ago that I needed a man to look after my office in the Rue Daunou of a morning, and he told me that in you I would find just the man I wanted."

"Hm!" grunted the fellow, very sullenly I thought. "I work for Farewell in the mornings. Why should he recommend me to you? Am I not giving satisfaction?"

"Perfect satisfaction," I rejoined urbanely; "that is just the point. Mr. Farewell desires to do you a good turn seeing that I offered to pay you twenty sous for your morning's work instead of the ten which you are getting from him."

I saw his eyes glisten at mention of the twenty sous.

"I'd best go and tell him then that I am taking on your work," he said; and his tone was no longer sullen now.

"Quite unnecessary," I rejoined. "I arranged everything with Mr. Farewell before I came to you. He has already found someone else to do his work, and I shall want you to be at my office by seven o'clock to-morrow morning. And," I added, for I am always cautious and judicious, and I now placed a piece of silver in his hand, "here are the first twenty sous on account."

He took the money and promptly became very civil, even obsequious. He not only accompanied me to the door, but all the way down the stairs, and assured me all the time that he would do his best to give me entire satisfaction.

I left my address with him, and sure enough, he turned up at the office the next morning at seven o'clock precisely.

Theodore had had my orders to direct him in his work, and I was left free to enact the second scene of the moving drama in which I was determined to play the hero and to ring down the curtain to the sound of the wedding bells.

3.

I took on the work of odd-job man at 65 Rue des Pyramides. Yes, I! Even I, who had sat in the private room of an emperor discussing the destinies of Europe.

But with a beautiful bride and one hundred thousand francs as my goal I would have worked in a coal mine or on the galleys for such a guerdon.

The task, I must tell you, was terribly irksome to a man of my sensibilities, endowed with an active mind and a vivid imagination. The dreary monotony of fetching water and fuel from below and polishing the boots of that arch-scoundrel Farewell would have made a less stout spirit quail. I had, of course, seen through the scoundrel's game at once. He had rendered Estelle quite helpless by keeping all her papers of identification and by withholding from her all the letters which, no doubt, the English lawyers wrote to her from time to time. Thus she was entirely in his power. But, thank heaven! only momentarily, for I, Hector Ratichon, argus-eyed, was on the watch. Now and then the monotony of my existence and the hardship of my task were relieved by a brief glimpse of Estelle or a smile of understanding from her lips; now and then she would contrive to murmur as she brushed past me while I was polishing the scoundrel's study floor, "Any luck yet?" And this quiet understanding between us gave me courage to go on with my task.

After three days I had conclusively made up my mind that Mr. Farewell kept his valuable papers in the drawer of the bureau in the study. After that I always kept a lump of wax ready for use in my pocket. On the fifth day I was very nearly caught trying to take an impression of the lock of the bureau drawer. On the seventh I succeeded, and took the impression over to a locksmith I knew of, and gave him an order to have a key made to fit it immediately. On the ninth day I had the key.

Then commenced a series of disappointments and of unprofitable days which would have daunted one less bold and less determined. I don't think that Farewell ever suspected me, but it is a fact that never once did he leave me alone in his study whilst I was at work there polishing the oak floor. And in the meanwhile I could see how he was pursuing my beautiful Estelle with his unwelcome attentions. At times I feared that he meant to abduct her; his was a powerful personality and she seemed like a little bird fighting against the fascination of a serpent. Latterly, too, an air of discouragement seemed to dwell upon her lovely face. I was half distraught with anxiety, and once or twice, whilst I knelt upon the hard floor, scrubbing and polishing as if my life depended on it, whilst he—the unscrupulous scoundrel—sat calmly at his desk, reading or writing, I used to feel as if the next moment I must attack him with my scrubbing-brush and knock him down senseless whilst I ransacked his drawers. My horror of anything approaching violence saved me from so foolish a step.

Then it was that in the hour of my blackest despair a flash of genius pierced through the darkness of my misery. For some days now Madame Dupont, Farewell's housekeeper, had been exceedingly affable to me. Every morning now, when I came to work, there was a cup of hot coffee waiting for me, and, when I left, a small parcel of something appetizing for me to take away.

"Hallo!" I said to myself one day, when, over a cup of coffee, I caught sight of her small, piggy eyes leering at me with an unmistakable expression of admiration. "Does salvation lie where I least expected it?"

For the moment I did nothing more than wink at the fat old thing, but the next morning I had my arm round her waist—a metre and a quarter, Sir, where it was tied in the middle—and had imprinted a kiss upon her glossy cheek. What that love-making cost me I cannot attempt to describe. Once Estelle came into the kitchen when I was staggering under a load of a hundred kilos sitting on my knee. The reproachful glance which she cast at me filled my soul with unspeakable sorrow.

But I was working for her dear sake; working that I might win her in the end.

A week later Mr. Farewell was absent from home for the evening. Estelle had retired to her room, and I was a welcome visitor in the kitchen, where Madame Dupont had laid out a regular feast for me. I had brought a couple of bottles of champagne with me and, what with the unaccustomed drink and the ogling and love-making to which I treated her, a hundred kilos of foolish womanhood was soon hopelessly addled and incapable. I managed to drag her to the sofa, where she remained quite still, with a beatific smile upon her podgy face, her eyes swimming in happy tears.

I had not a moment to lose. The very next minute I was in the study and with a steady hand was opening the drawers of the bureau and turning over the letters and papers which I found therein.

Suddenly an exclamation of triumph escaped my lips.

I held a packet in my hand on which was written in a clear hand: "The papers of Mlle. Estelle Bachelier." A brief examination of the packet sufficed. It consisted of a number of letters written in English, which language I only partially understand, but they all bore the same signature, "John Pike and Sons, solicitors," and the address was at the top, "168 Cornhill, London." It also contained my Estelle's birth certificate, her mother's marriage certificate, and her police registration card.

I was rapt in the contemplation of my own ingenuity in having thus brilliantly attained my goal, when a stealthy noise in the next room roused me from my trance and brought up vividly to my mind the awful risks which I was running at this moment. I turned like an animal at bay to see Estelle's beautiful face peeping at me through the half-open door.

"Hist!" she whispered. "Have you got the papers?"

I waved the packet triumphantly. She, excited and adorable, stepped briskly into the room.

"Let me see," she murmured excitedly.

But I, emboldened by success, cried gaily:

"Not till I have received compensation for all that I have done and endured."

"Compensation?"

"In the shape of a kiss."

Oh! I won't say that she threw herself in my arms then and there. No, no! She demurred. All young girls, it seems, demur under the circumstances; but she was adorable, coy and tender in turns, pouting and coaxing, and playing like a kitten till she had taken the papers from me and, with a woman's natural curiosity, had turned the English letters over and over, even though she could not read a word of them.

Then, Sir, in the midst of her innocent frolic and at the very moment when I was on the point of snatching the kiss which she had so tantalizingly denied me, we heard the opening and closing of the front door.

Mr. Farewell had come home, and there was no other egress from the study save the sitting-room, which in its turn had no other egress but the door leading into the very passage where even now Mr. Farewell was standing, hanging up his hat and cloak on the rack.

4.

We stood hand in hand—Estelle and I—fronting the door through which Mr. Farewell would presently appear.

"To-night we fly together," I declared.

"Where to?" she whispered.

"Can you go to the woman at your former lodgings?"

"Yes!"

"Then I will take you there to-night. To-morrow we will be married before the Procureur du Roi; in the evening we leave for England."

"Yes, yes!" she murmured.

"When he comes in I'll engage him in conversation," I continued hurriedly. "You make a dash for the door and run downstairs as fast as you can. I'll follow as quickly as may be and meet you under the porte-cochere."

She had only just time to nod assent when the door which gave on the sitting-room was pushed open, and Farewell, unconscious at first of our presence, stepped quietly into the room.

"Estelle," he cried, more puzzled than angry when he suddenly caught sight of us both, "what are you doing here with that lout?"

I was trembling with excitement—not fear, of course, though Farewell was a powerful-looking man, a head taller than I was. I stepped boldly forward, covering the adored one with my body.

"The lout," I said with calm dignity, "has frustrated the machinations of a knave. To-morrow I go to England in order to place Mademoiselle Estelle Bachelier under the protection of her legal guardians, Messieurs Pike and Sons, solicitors, of London."

He gave a cry of rage, and before I could retire to some safe entrenchment behind the table or the sofa, he was upon me like a mad dog. He had me by the throat, and I had rolled backwards down on to the floor, with him on the top of me, squeezing the breath out of me till I verily thought that my last hour had come. Estelle had run out of the room like a startled hare. This, of course, was in accordance with my instructions to her, but I could not help wishing then that she had been less obedient and somewhat more helpful.

As it was, I was beginning to feel a mere worm in the grip of that savage scoundrel, whose face I could perceive just above me, distorted with passion, whilst hoarse ejaculations escaped his trembling lips:

"You meddlesome fool! You oaf! You toad! This for your interference!" he added as he gave me a vigorous punch on the head.

I felt my senses reeling. My head was swimming, my eyes no longer could see distinctly. It seemed as if an unbearable pressure upon my chest would finally squeeze the last breath out of my body.

I was trying to remember the prayers I used to murmur at my mother's knee, for verily I thought that I was dying, when suddenly, through my fading senses, came the sound of a long, hoarse cry, whilst the floor was shaken as with an earthquake. The next moment the pressure on my chest seemed to relax. I could hear Farewell's voice uttering language such as it would be impossible for me to put on record; and through it all hoarse and convulsive cries of: "You shan't hurt him—you limb of Satan, you!"

Gradually strength returned to me. I could see as well as hear, and what I saw filled me with wonder and with pride. Wonder at Ma'ame Dupont's pluck! Pride in that her love for me had given such power to her mighty arms! Aroused from her slumbers by the sound of the scuffle, she had run to the study, only to find me in deadly peril of my life. Without a second's hesitation she had rushed on Farewell, seized him by the collar, pulled him away from me, and then thrown the whole weight of her hundred kilos upon him, rendering him helpless.

Ah, woman! lovely, selfless woman! My heart a prey to remorse, in that I could not remain in order to thank my plucky deliverer, I nevertheless finally struggled to my feet and fled from the apartment and down the stairs, never drawing breath till I felt Estelle's hand resting confidingly upon my arm.

5.

I took her to the house where she used to lodge, and placed her under the care of the kind concierge who was Theodore's aunt. Then I, too, went home, determined to get a good night's rest. The morning would be a busy one for me. There would be the special licence to get, the cure of St. Jacques to interview, the religious ceremony to arrange for, and the places to book on the stagecoach for Boulogne *en route* for England—and fortune.

I was supremely happy and slept the sleep of the just. I was up betimes and started on my round of business at eight o'clock the next morning. I was a little troubled about money, because when I had paid for the licence and given to the cure the required fee for the religious service and ceremony, I had only five francs left out of the hundred which the adored one had given me. However, I booked the seats on the stage-coach and determined to trust to luck. Once Estelle was my wife, all money care would be at an end, since no power on earth could stand between me and the hundred thousand francs, the happy goal for which I had so ably striven.

The marriage ceremony was fixed for eleven o'clock, and it was just upon ten when, at last, with a light heart and springy step, I ran up the dingy staircase which led to the adored one's apartments. I knocked at the door. It was opened by a young man, who with a smile courteously bade me enter. I felt a little bewildered—and slightly annoyed. My Estelle should not receive visits from young men at this hour. I pushed past the intruder in the passage, and walked boldly into the room beyond.

Estelle was sitting upon the sofa, her eyes bright, her mouth smiling, a dimple in each cheek. I approached her with outstretched arms, but she paid no heed to me, and turned to the young man, who had followed me into the room.

"Adrien," she said, "this is kind M. Ratichon, who at risk of his life obtained for us all my papers of identification and also the valuable name and address of the English lawyers."

"Monsieur," added the young man as he extended his hand to me, "Estelle and I will remain eternally your debtors."

I struck at the hand which he had so impudently held out to me and turned to Estelle with my usual dignified calm, but with wrath expressed in every line of my face.

"Estelle," I said, "what is the meaning of this?"

"Oh," she retorted with one of her provoking smiles, "you must not call me Estelle, you know, or Adrien will smack your face. We are indeed grateful to you, my good M. Ratichon," she continued more seriously, "and though I only promised you another hundred francs when your work for me was completed, my husband and I have decided to give you a thousand francs in view of the risks which you ran on our behalf."

"Your husband!" I stammered.

"I was married to M. Adrien Cazalès a month ago," she said, "but we had perforce to keep our marriage a secret, because Mr. Farewell once vowed to me that unless I became his wife he would destroy all my papers of identification, and then—even if I ever succeeded in discovering who were the English lawyers who had charge of my father's money—I could never prove it to them that I and no one else was entitled to it. But for you, dear M. Ratichon," added the cruel and shameless one, "I should indeed never have succeeded."

In the midst of this overwhelming cataclysm I am proud to say that I retained mastery over my rage and contrived to say with perfect calm:

"But why have deceived me, Mademoiselle? Why have kept your marriage a secret from me? Was I not toiling and working and risking my life for you?"

"And would you have worked quite so enthusiastically for me," queried the false one archly, "if I had told you everything?"

I groaned. Perhaps she was right. I don't know.

I took the thousand francs and never saw M. and Mme. Cazalès again.

But I met Ma'ame Dupont by accident soon after. She has left Mr. Farewell's service.

She still weighs one hundred kilos.

I often call on her of an evening.

Ah, well!

CHAPTER III

ON THE BRINK

1.

You would have thought that after the shameful way in which Theodore treated me in the matter of the secret treaty that I would then and there have turned him out of doors, sent him back to grub for scraps out of the gutter, and hardened my heart once and for all against that snake in the grass whom I had nurtured in my bosom.

But, as no doubt you have remarked ere this, I have been burdened by Nature with an over-sensitive heart. It is a burden, my dear Sir, and though I have suffered inexpressibly under it, I nevertheless agree with the English poet, George Crabbe, whose works I have read with a great deal of pleasure and profit in the original tongue, and who avers in one of his inimitable "Tales" that it is "better to love amiss than nothing to have loved."

Not that I loved Theodore, you understand? But he and I had shared so many ups and downs together of late that I was loath to think of him as reduced to begging his bread in the streets. Then I kept him by me, for I thought that he might at times be useful to me in my business.

I kept him to my hurt, as you will presently see.

In those days—I am now speaking of the time immediately following the Restoration of our beloved King Louis XVIII to the throne of his forbears— Parisian society was, as it were, divided into two distinct categories: those who had become impoverished by the revolution and the wars of the Empire, and those who had made their fortunes thereby. Among the former was M. le Marquis de Firmin-Latour, a handsome young officer of cavalry; and among the latter was one Mauruss Mosenstein, a usurer of the Jewish persuasion, whose wealth was reputed in millions, and who had a handsome daughter biblically named Rachel, who a year ago had become Madame la Marquise de Firmin-Latour.

From the first moment that this brilliant young couple appeared upon the firmament of Parisian society I took a keen interest in all their doings. In those days, you understand, it was in the essence of my business to know as much as possible of the private affairs of people in their position, and instinct had at once told me that in the case of M. le Marquis de Firmin-Latour such knowledge might prove very remunerative.

Thus I very soon found out that M. le Marquis had not a single louis of his own to bless himself with, and that it was Papa Mosenstein's millions that kept up the young people's magnificent establishment in the Rue de Grammont.

I also found out that Mme. la Marquise was some dozen years older than Monsieur, and that she had been a widow when she married him. There were rumours that her first marriage had not been a happy one. The husband, M. le Compte de Naquet, had been a gambler and a spendthrift, and had dissipated as much of his wife's fortune as he could lay his hands on, until one day he went off on a voyage to America, or goodness knows where, and was never heard of again. Mme. la Comtesse, as she then was, did not grieve over her loss; indeed, she returned to the bosom of her family, and her father—a shrewd usurer, who had amassed an enormous fortune during the wars—succeeded, with the aid of his apparently bottomless moneybags, in having his first son-in-law declared deceased by Royal decree, so as to enable the beautiful Rachel to contract another, yet more brilliant alliance, as far as name and lineage were concerned, with the Marquis de Firmin-Latour.

Indeed, I learned that the worthy Israelite's one passion was the social advancement of his daughter, whom he worshipped. So, as soon as the marriage was consummated and the young people were home from their honeymoon, he fitted up for their use the most extravagantly sumptuous apartment Paris had ever seen. Nothing seemed too good or too luxurious for Mme. la Marquise de Firmin-Latour. He desired her to cut a brilliant figure in Paris society—nay, to be the Ville Lumiere's brightest and most particular star. After the town house he bought a chateau in the country, horses and carriages, which he placed at the disposal of the young couple; he kept up an army of servants for them, and replenished their cellars with the choicest wines. He threw money about for diamonds and pearls which his daughter wore, and paid all his son-in-law's tailors' and shirt-makers' bills. But always the money was his, you understand? The house in Paris was his, so was the chateau on the Loire; he lent them to his daughter. He lent her the diamonds, and the carriages, and the boxes at the opera and the Français. But here his generosity ended. He had been deceived in his daughter's first husband; some of the money which he had given her had gone to pay the gambling debts of an unscrupulous spendthrift. He was determined that this should not occur again. A man might spend his wife's money—indeed, the law placed most of it at his disposal in those days—but he could not touch or mortgage one sou that belonged to his father-in-law. And, strangely enough, Mme. la Marquise de Firmin-Latour acquiesced and aided her father in his determination. Whether it was the Jewish blood in her, or merely obedience to old Mosenstein's whim, it were impossible to say. Certain it is that out of the lavish pin-money which her father gave her as a free gift from time to time, she only doled out a meagre allowance to her husband, and although she had everything she wanted, M. le Marquis on his side had often less than twenty francs in his pocket.

A very humiliating position, you will admit, Sir, for a dashing young cavalry officer. Often have I seen him gnawing his finger-nails with rage when, at the end of a copious dinner in one of the fashionable restaurants—where I myself was engaged in a business capacity to keep an eye on possibly light-fingered customers—it would be Mme. la Marquise who paid the bill, even gave the pourboire to the waiter. At such times my heart would be filled with pity for his misfortunes, and, in my own proud and lofty independence, I felt that I did not envy him his wife's millions.

Of course, he borrowed from every usurer in the city for as long as they would lend him any money; but now he was up to his eyes in debt, and there was not a Jew inside France who would have lent him one hundred francs.

You see, his precarious position was as well known as were his extravagant tastes and the obstinate parsimoniousness of M. Mosenstein.

But such men as M. le Marquis de Firmin-Latour, you understand, Sir, are destined by Nature first and by fortuitous circumstances afterwards to become the clients of men of ability like myself. I knew that sooner or later the elegant young soldier would be forced to seek the advice of someone wiser than himself, for indeed his present situation could not last much longer. It would soon be "sink" with him, for he could no longer "swim."

And I was determined that when that time came he should turn to me as the drowning man turns to the straw.

So where M. le Marquis went in public I went, when possible. I was biding my time, and wisely too, as you will judge.

2.

Then one day our eyes met: not in a fashionable restaurant, I may tell you, but in a discreet one situated on the slopes of Montmartre. I was there alone, sipping a cup of coffee after a frugal dinner. I had drifted in there chiefly because I had quite accidentally caught sight of M. le Marquis de Firmin-Latour walking arm-in-arm up the Rue Lepic with a lady who was both youthful and charming—a well-known dancer at the opera. Presently I saw him turn into that discreet little restaurant, where, in very truth, it was not likely that Mme. la Marquise would follow him. But I did. What made me do it, I cannot say; but for some time now it had been my wish to make the personal acquaintance of M. de Firmin-Latour, and I lost no opportunity which might help me to attain this desire.

Somehow the man interested me. His social and financial position was peculiar, you will admit, and here, methought, was the beginning of an adventure which might prove the turning-point in his career and . . . my opportunity. I was not wrong, as you will presently see. Whilst silently eating my simple dinner, I watched M. de Firmin-Latour.

He had started the evening by being very gay; he had ordered champagne and a succulent meal, and chatted light-heartedly with his companion, until presently three young women, flashily dressed, made noisy irruption into the restaurant.

M. de Firmin-Latour's friend hailed them, introduced them to him, and soon he was host, not to one lady, but to four, and instead of two dinners he had to order five, and more champagne, and then dessert—peaches, strawberries, bonbons, liqueurs, flowers, and what not, until I could see that the bill which presently he would be called upon to pay would amount to far more than his quarterly allowance from Mme. la Marquise, far more, presumably, than he had in his pocket at the present moment.

My brain works with marvellous rapidity, as you know. Already I had made up my mind to see the little comedy through to the end, and I watched with a good deal of interest and some pity the clouds of anxiety gathering over M. de Firmin-Latour's brow.

The dinner party lasted some considerable time; then the inevitable cataclysm occurred. The ladies were busy chattering and rouging their lips when the bill was presented. They affected to see and hear nothing: it is a way ladies have when dinner has to be paid for; but I saw and heard everything. The waiter stood by, silent and obsequious at first, whilst M. le Marquis hunted through all his pockets. Then there was some whispered colloquy, and the waiter's attitude lost something of its correct dignity. After that the proprietor was called, and the whispered colloquy degenerated into altercation, whilst the ladies—not at all unaware of the situation—giggled amongst themselves. Finally, M. le Marquis offered a promissory note, which was refused.

Then it was that our eyes met. M. de Firmin-Latour had flushed to the roots of his hair. His situation was indeed desperate, and my opportunity had come. With consummate sang-froid, I advanced towards the agitated group composed of M. le Marquis, the proprietor, and the head waiter. I glanced at the bill, the cause of all this turmoil, which reposed on a metal salver in the head waiter's hand, and with a brief:

"If M. le Marquis will allow me . . ." I produced my pocket-book.

The bill was for nine hundred francs.

At first M. le Marquis thought that I was about to pay it—and so did the proprietor of the establishment, who made a movement as if he would lie down on the floor and lick my boots. But not so. To begin with, I did not happen to possess nine hundred francs, and if I did, I should not Have been fool enough to lend them to this young scapegrace. No! What I did was to extract from my notebook a card, one of a series which I always keep by me in case of an emergency like the present one. It bore the legend: "Comte Hercule de Montjoie, secrétaire particulier de M. le Duc d'Otrante," and below it the address, "Palais du Commissariat de Police, 12 Quai d'Orsay." This card I presented with a graceful flourish of the arm to the proprietor of the establishment, whilst I said with that lofty self-assurance which is one of my finest attributes and which I have never seen equalled:

"M. le Marquis is my friend. I will be guarantee for this trifling amount."

The proprietor and head waiter stammered excuses. Private secretary of M. le Duc d'Otrante! Think of it! It is not often that such personages deign to frequent the .restaurants of Montmartre. M. le Marquis, on the other hand, looked completely bewildered, whilst I, taking advantage of the situation, seized him familiarly by the arm, and leading him toward the door, I said with condescending urbanity:

"One word with you, my dear Marquis. It is so long since we have met."

I bowed to the ladies.

"Mesdames," I said, and was gratified to see that they followed my dramatic exit with eyes of appreciation and of wonder. The proprietor himself offered me my hat, and a moment or two later M. de Firmin-Latour and I were out together in the Rue Lepic.

"My dear Comte," he said as soon as he had recovered his breath, "how can I think you? . . ."

"Not now, Monsieur, not now," I replied. "You have only just time to make your way as quickly as you can back to your palace in the Rue de Grammont before our friend the proprietor discovers the several mistakes which he has made in the past few minutes and vents his wrath upon your fair guests."

"You are right," he rejoined lightly. "But I will have the pleasure to call on you to-morrow at the Palais du Commissariat."

"Do no such thing, Monsieur le Marquis," I retorted with a pleasant laugh. "You would not find me there."

"But—" he stammered.

"But," I broke in with my wonted business-like and persuasive manner, "if you think that I have conducted this delicate affair for you with tact and discretion, then, in your own interest I should advise you to call on me at my private office, No. 96 Rue Daunou. Hector Ratichon, at your service."

He appeared more bewildered than ever.

"Rue Daunou," he murmured. "Ratichon!"

"Private inquiry and confidential agent," I rejoined. "My brains are at your service should you desire to extricate yourself from the humiliating financial position in which it has been my good luck to find you, and yours to meet with me."

With that I left him, Sir, to walk away or stay as he pleased. As for me, I went quickly down the street. I felt that the situation was absolutely perfect; to have spoken another word might have spoilt it. Moreover, there was no knowing how soon the proprietor of that humble hostelry would begin to have doubts as to the identity of the private secretary of M. le Duc d'Otrante. So I was best out of the way.

3.

The very next day M. le Marquis de Firmin-Latour called upon me at my office in the Rue Daunou. Theodore let him in, and the first thing that struck me about him was his curt, haughty manner and the look of disdain wherewith he regarded the humble appointments of my business premises. He himself was magnificently dressed, I may tell you. His bottle-green coat was of the finest cloth and the most perfect cut I had ever seen. His kerseymere pantaloons fitted him without a wrinkle. He wore gloves, he carried a muff of priceless zibeline, and in his cravat there was a diamond the size of a broad bean.

He also carried a malacca cane, which he deposited upon my desk, and a gold-rimmed spy-glass which, with a gesture of supreme affectation, he raised to his eye.

"Now, M. Hector Ratichon," he said abruptly, "perhaps you will be good enough to explain."

I had risen when he entered. But now I sat down again and coolly pointed to the best chair in the room.

"Will you give yourself the trouble to sit down, M. le Marquis?" I riposted blandly.

He called me names—rude names! but I took no notice of that . . . and he sat down.

"Now!" he said once more.

"What is it you desire to know, M. le Marquis?" I queried.

"Why you interfered in my affairs last night?"

"Do you complain?" I asked.

"No," he admitted reluctantly, "but I don't understand your object."

"My object was to serve you then," I rejoined quietly, "and later."

"What do you mean by 'later'?"

"To-day," I replied, "to-morrow; whenever your present position becomes absolutely unendurable."

"It is that now," he said with a savage oath.

"I thought as much," was my curt comment.

"And do you mean to assert," he went on more earnestly, "that you can find a way out of it?"

"If you desire it—yes!" I said.

"How?"

He drew his chair nearer to my desk, and I leaned forward, with my elbows on the table, the finger-tips of one hand in contact with those of the other.

"Let us begin by reviewing the situation, shall we, Monsieur?" I began.

"If you wish," he said curtly.

"You are a gentleman of refined, not to say luxurious tastes, who finds himself absolutely without means to gratify them. Is that so?"

He nodded.

"You have a wife and a father-in-law who, whilst lavishing costly treasures upon you, leave you in a humiliating dependence on them for actual money."

Again he nodded approvingly.

"Human nature," I continued with gentle indulgence, "being what it is, you pine after what you do not possess—namely, money. Houses, equipages, servants, even good food and wine, are nothing to you beside that earnest desire for money that you can call your own, and which, if only you had it, you could spend at your pleasure."

"To the point, man, to the point!" he broke in impatiently.

"One moment, M. le Marquis, and I have done. But first of all, with your permission, shall we also review the assets in your life which we will have to use in order to arrive at the gratification of your earnest wish?"

"Assets? What do you mean?"

"The means to our end. You want money; we must find the means to get it for you."

"I begin to understand," he said, and drew his chair another inch or two closer to me.

"Firstly, M. le Marquis," I resumed, and now my voice had become earnest and incisive, "firstly you have a wife, then you have a father-in-law whose wealth is beyond the dreams of humble people like myself, and whose one great passion in life is the social position of the daughter whom he worships. Now," I added, and with the tip of my little finger I touched the sleeve of my aristocratic client, "here at once is your first asset. Get at the money-bags of papa by threatening the social position of his daughter."

Whereupon my young gentleman jumped to his feet and swore and abused me for a mudlark and a muckworm and I don't know what. He seized his malacca cane and threatened me with it, and asked me how the devil I dared thus to speak of Mme. la Marquise de Firmin-Latour. He cursed, and he stormed and he raved of his sixteen quarterings and of my loutishness. He did everything in fact except walk out of the room.

I let him go on quite quietly. It was part of his programme, and we had to go through the performance. As soon as he gave me the chance of putting in a word edgeways I rejoined quietly:

"We are not going to hurt Madame la Marquise, Monsieur; and if you do not want the money, let us say no more about it."

Whereupon he calmed down; after a while he sat down again, this time with his cane between his knees and its ivory knob between his teeth.

"Go on," he said curtly.

Nor did he interrupt me again whilst I expounded my scheme to him—one that, mind you, I had evolved during the night, knowing well that I should receive his visit during the day; and I flatter myself that no finer scheme for the bleeding of a parsimonious usurer was ever devised by any man.

If it succeeded—and there was no reason why it should not—M. de Firmin-Latour would pocket a cool half-million, whilst I, sir, the brain that had devised the whole scheme, pronounced myself satisfied with the paltry emolument of one hundred thousand francs, out of which, remember, I should have to give Theodore a considerable sum.

We talked it all over, M. le Marquis and I, the whole afternoon. I may tell you at once that he was positively delighted with the plan, and then and there gave me one hundred francs out of his own meagre purse for my preliminary expenses.

The next morning we began work.

I had begged M. le Marquis to find the means of bringing me a few scraps of the late M. le Comte de Naquet's—Madame la Marquise's first husband—handwriting. This, fortunately, he was able to do. They were a few valueless notes penned at different times by the deceased gentleman and which, luckily for us all, Madame had not thought it worth while to keep under lock and key.

I think I told you before, did I not? what a marvellous expert I am in every kind of calligraphy, and soon I had a letter ready which was to represent the first fire in the exciting war which we were about to wage against an obstinate lady and a parsimonious usurer.

My identity securely hidden under the disguise of a commissionnaire, I took that letter to Mme. la Marquise de Firmin-Latour's sumptuous abode in the Rue de Grammont.

M. le Marquis, you understand, had in the meanwhile been thoroughly primed in the rôle which he was to play; as for Theodore, I thought it best for the moment to dispense with his aid.

The success of our first skirmish surpassed our expectations.

Ten minutes after the letter had been taken upstairs to Mme. la Marquise, one of the maids, on going past her mistress's door, was startled to hear cries and moans proceeding from Madame's room. She entered and found Madame lying on the sofa, her face buried in the cushions, and sobbing and screaming in a truly terrifying manner. The maid applied the usual restoratives, and after a while Madame became more calm and at once very curtly ordered the maid out of the room.

M. le Marquis, on being apprised of this mysterious happening, was much distressed; he hurried to his wife's apartments, and was as gentle and loving with her as he had been in the early days of their honeymoon. But throughout the whole of that evening, and, indeed, for the next two days, all the explanation that he could get from Madame herself was that she had a headache and that the letter which she had received that afternoon was of no consequence and had nothing to do with her migraine.

But clearly the beautiful Rachel was extraordinarily agitated. At night she did not sleep, but would pace up and down her apartments in a state bordering on frenzy, which of course caused M. le Marquis a great deal of anxiety and of sorrow.

Finally, on the Friday morning it seemed as if Madame could contain herself no longer. She threw herself into her husband's arms and blurted out the whole truth. M. le Comte de Naquet, her first husband, who had been declared drowned at sea, and therefore officially deceased by Royal decree, was not dead at all. Madame had received a letter from him wherein he told her that he had indeed suffered shipwreck, then untold misery on a desert island for three years, until he had been rescued by a passing vessel, and finally been able, since he was destitute, to work his way back to France and to Paris. Here he had lived for the past few months as best he could, trying to collect together a little money so as to render himself presentable before his wife, whom he had never ceased to love.

Inquiries discreetly conducted had revealed the terrible truth, that Madame had been faithless to him, had light-heartedly assumed the death of her husband, and had contracted what was nothing less than a bigamous marriage. Now he, M. de Naquet, standing on his rights as Rachel Mosenstein's only lawful husband, demanded that she should return to him, and as a prelude to a permanent and amicable understanding, she was to call at three o'clock precisely on the following Friday at No. 96 Rue Daunou, where their reconciliation and reunion was to take place.

The letter announcing this terrible news and making this preposterous demand she now placed in the hands of M. le Marquis, who at first was horrified and thunderstruck, and appeared quite unable to deal with the situation or to tender advice. For Madame it meant complete social ruin, of course, and she herself declared that she would never survive such a scandal. Her tears and her misery made the loving heart of M. le Marquis bleed in sympathy. He did all he could to console and comfort the lady, whom, alas! he could no longer look upon as his wife. Then, gradually, both he and she became more composed. It was necessary above all things to make sure that Madame was not being victimized by an impostor, and for this purpose M. le Marquis generously offered himself as a disinterested friend and adviser. He offered to go himself to the Rue Daunou at the hour appointed and to do his best to induce M. le Comte de Naquet—if indeed he existed—to forgo his rights on the lady who had so innocently taken on the name and hand of M. le Marquis de Firmin-Latour. Somewhat more calm, but still unconsoled, the beautiful Rachel accepted this generous offer. I believe that she even found five thousand francs in her privy purse which was to be offered to M. de Naquet in exchange for a promise never to worry Mme. la Marquise again with his presence. But this I have never been able to ascertain with any finality. Certain it is that when at three o'clock on that same afternoon M. de Firmin-Latour presented himself at my office, he did not offer me a share in any five thousand francs, though he spoke to me about the money, adding that he thought it would look well if he were to give it back to Madame, and to tell her that M. de Naquet had rejected so paltry a sum with disdain.

I thought such a move unnecessary, and we argued about it rather warmly, and in the end he went away, as I say, without offering me any share in the emolument. Whether he did put his project into execution or not I never knew. He told me that he did. After that there followed for me, Sir, many days, nay, weeks, of anxiety and of strenuous work. Mme. la Marquise received several more letters from the supposititious M. de Naquet, any one of which would have landed me, Sir, in a vessel bound for New Caledonia. The discarded husband became more and more insistent as time went on, and finally sent an ultimatum to Madame saying that he was tired of perpetual interviews with M. le Marquis de Firmin-Latour, whose right to interfere in the matter he now wholly denied, and that he was quite determined to claim his lawful wife before the whole world.

Madame la Marquise, in the meanwhile, had passed from one fit of hysterics into another. She denied her door to everyone and lived in the strictest seclusion in her beautiful apartment of the Rue de Grammont. Fortunately this all occurred in the early autumn, when the absence of such a society star from fashionable gatherings was not as noticeable as it otherwise would have been.

But clearly we were working up for the climax, which occurred in the way I am about to relate.

4.

Ah, my dear Sir, when after all these years I think of my adventure with that abominable Marquis, righteous and noble indignation almost strikes me dumb. To think that with my own hands and brains I literally put half a million into that man's pocket, and that he repaid me with the basest ingratitude, almost makes me lose my faith in human nature. Theodore, of course, I could punish, and did so adequately; and where my chastisement failed, Fate herself put the finishing touch.

But M. de Firmin-Latour . . .!

However, you shall judge for yourself.

As I told you, we now made ready for the climax; and that climax, Sir, I can only describe as positively gorgeous. We began by presuming that Mme. la Marquise had now grown tired of incessant demands for interviews and small doles of money, and that she would be willing to offer a considerable sum to her first and only lawful husband in exchange for a firm guarantee that he would never trouble her again as long as she lived.

We fixed the sum at half a million francs, and the guarantee was to take the form of a deed duly executed by a notary of repute and signed by the supposititious Comte de Naquet. A letter embodying the demand and offering the guarantee was thereupon duly sent to Mme. la Marquise, and she, after the usual attack of hysterics, duly confided the matter to M. de Firmin-Latour.

The consultation between husband and wife on the deplorable subject was touching in the extreme; and I will give that abominable Marquis credit for playing his rôle in a masterly manner. At first he declared to his dear Rachel that he did not know what to suggest, for in truth she had nothing like half a million on which she could lay her hands. To speak of this awful pending scandal to Papa Mosenstein was not to be thought of. He was capable of repudiating the daughter altogether who was bringing such obloquy upon herself and would henceforth be of no use to him as a society star.

As for himself in this terrible emergency, he, of course, had less than nothing, or his entire fortune would be placed—if he had one—at the feet of his beloved Rachel. To think that he was on the point of losing her was more than he could bear, and the idea that she would soon become the talk of every gossip-monger in society, and mayhap be put in prison for bigamy, wellnigh drove him crazy.

What could be done in this awful perplexity he for one could not think, unless indeed his dear Rachel were willing to part with some of her jewellery; but no! he could not think of allowing her to make such a sacrifice.

Whereupon Madame, like a drowning man, or rather woman, catching at a straw, bethought her of her emeralds. They were historic gems, once the property of the Empress Marie-Thérèse, and had been given to her on her second marriage by her adoring father. No, no! she would never miss them; she seldom wore them, for they were heavy and more valuable than elegant, and she was quite sure that at the Mont de Piété they would lend her five hundred thousand francs on them. Then gradually they could be redeemed before papa had become aware of their temporary disappearance. Madame would save the money out of the liberal allowance she received from him for pin-money. Anything, anything was preferable to this awful doom which hung over her head.

But even so M. le Marquis demurred. The thought of his proud and fashionable Rachel going to the Mont de Piété to pawn her own jewels was not to be thought of. She would be seen, recognized, and the scandal would be as bad and worse than anything that loomed on the black horizon of her fate at this hour.

What was to be done? What was to be done?

Then M. le Marquis had a brilliant idea. He knew of a man, a very reliable, trustworthy man, attorney-at-law by profession, and therefore a man of repute, who was often obliged in the exercise of his profession to don various disguises when tracking criminals in the outlying quarters of Paris. M. le Marquis, putting all pride and dignity nobly aside in the interests of his adored Rachel, would borrow one of these disguises and himself go to the Mont de Piété with the emeralds, obtain the five hundred thousand francs, and remit them to the man whom he hated most in all the world, in exchange for the aforementioned guarantee.

Madame la Marquise, overcome with gratitude, threw herself, in the midst of a flood of tears, into the arms of the man whom she no longer dared to call her husband, and so the matter was settled for the moment. M. le Marquis undertook to have the deed of guarantee drafted by the same notary of repute whom he knew, and, if Madame approved of it, the emeralds would then be converted into money, and the interview with M. le Comte de Naquet fixed for Wednesday, October 10th, at some convenient place, subsequently to be determined on—in all probability at the bureau of that same ubiquitous attorney-at-law, M. Hector Ratichon, at 96 Rue Daunon.

All was going on excellently well, as you observe. I duly drafted the deed, and M. de Firmin-Latour showed it to Madame for her approval. It was so simply and so comprehensively worded that she expressed herself thoroughly satisfied with it, whereupon M. le Marquis asked her to write to her shameful persecutor in order to fix the date and hour for the exchange of the money against the deed duly signed and witnessed. M. le Marquis had always been the intermediary for her letters, you understand, and for the small sums of money which she had sent from time to time to the factitious M. de Naquet; now he was to be entrusted with the final negotiations which, though at a heavy cost, would bring security and happiness once more in the sumptuous palace of the Rue de Grammont.

Then it was that the first little hitch occurred. Mme. la Marquise—whether prompted thereto by a faint breath of suspicion, or merely by natural curiosity—altered her mind about the appointment. She decided that M. le Marquis, having pledged the emeralds, should bring the money to her, and she herself would go to the bureau of M. Hector Ratichon in the Rue Daunou, there to meet M. de Naquet, whom she had not seen for seven years, but who had once been very dear to her, and herself fling in his face the five hundred thousand francs, the price of his silence and of her peace of mind.

At once, as you perceive, the situation became delicate. To have demurred, or uttered more than a casual word of objection, would in the case of M. le Marquis have been highly impolitic. He felt that at once, the moment he raised his voice in protest: and when Madame declared herself determined he immediately gave up arguing the point.

The trouble was that we had so very little time wherein to formulate new plans. Monsieur was to go the very next morning to the Mont de Piété to negotiate the emeralds, and the interview with the fabulous M. de Naquet was to take place a couple of hours later; and it was now three o'clock in the afternoon.

As soon as M. de Firmin-Latour was able to leave his wife, he came round to my office. He appeared completely at his wits' end, not knowing what to do.

"If my wife," he said, "insists on a personal interview with de Naquet, who does not exist, our entire scheme falls to the ground. Nay, worse! for I shall be driven to concoct some impossible explanation for the non-appearance of that worthy, and heaven only knows if I shall succeed in wholly allaying my wife's suspicions.

"Ah!" he added with a sigh, "it is doubly hard to have seen fortune so near one's reach and then to see it dashed away at one fell swoop by the relentless hand of Fate."

Not one word, you observe, of gratitude to me or of recognition of the subtle mind that had planned and devised the whole scheme.

But, Sir, it is at the hour of supreme crises like the present one that Hector Ratichon's genius soars up to the empyrean. It became great, Sir; nothing short of great; and even the marvellous schemes of the Italian Macchiavelli paled before the ingenuity which I now displayed.

Half an hour's reflection had sufficed. I had made my plans, and I had measured the full length of the terrible risks which I ran. Among these New Caledonia was the least. But I chose to take the risks, Sir; my genius could not stoop to measuring the costs of its flight. While M. de Firmin-Latour alternately raved and lamented I had already planned and contrived. As I say, we had very little time: a few hours wherein to render ourselves worthy of Fortune's smiles. And this is what I planned.

You tell me that you were not in Paris during the year 1816 of which I speak. If you had been, you would surely recollect the sensation caused throughout the entire city by the disappearance of M. le Marquis de Firmin-Latour, one of the most dashing young officers in society and one of its acknowledged leaders. It was the 10th day of October. M. le Marquis had breakfasted in the company of Madame at nine o'clock. A couple of hours later he went out, saying he would be home for déjeuner. Madame clearly expected him, for his place was laid, and she ordered the déjeuner to be kept back over an hour in anticipation of his return. But he did not come. The afternoon wore on and he did not come. Madame sat down at two o'clock to déjeuner alone. She told the major-domo that M. le Marquis was detained in town and might not be home for some time. But the major-domo declared that Madame's voice, as she told him this, sounded tearful and forced, and that she ate practically nothing, refusing one succulent dish after another.

The staff of servants was thus kept on tenterhooks all day, and when the shadows of evening began to draw in, the theory was started in the kitchen that M. le Marquis had either met with an accident or been foully murdered. No one, however, dared speak of this to Madame la Marquise, who had locked herself up in her room in the early part of the afternoon, and since then had refused to see anyone. The major-domo was now at his wits' end. He felt that in a measure the responsibility of the household rested upon his shoulders. Indeed he would have taken it upon himself to apprise M. Mauruss Mosenstein of the terrible happenings, only that the worthy gentleman was absent from Paris just then.

Mme. la Marquise remained shut up in her room until past eight o'clock. Then she ordered dinner to be served and made pretence of sitting down to it; but again the major-domo declared that she ate nothing, whilst subsequently the confidential maid who had undressed her vowed that Madame had spent the whole night walking up and down the room.

Thus two agonizing days went by; agonizing they were to everybody. Madame la Marquise became more and more agitated, more and more hysterical as time went on, and the servants could not help but notice this, even though she made light of the whole affair, and desperate efforts to control herself. The heads of her household, the major-domo, the confidential maid, the chef de cuisine, did venture to drop a hint or two as to the possibility of an accident or of foul play, and the desirability of consulting the police; but Madame would not hear a word of it; she became very angry at the suggestion, and declared that she was perfectly well aware of M. le Marquis's whereabouts, that he was well and would return home almost immediately.

As was only natural, tongues presently began to wag. Soon it was common talk in Paris that M. le Marquis de Firmin-Latour had disappeared from his home and that Madame was trying to put a bold face upon the occurrence. There were surmises and there was gossip— oh! interminable and long-winded gossip! Minute circumstances in connexion with M. le Marquis's private life and Mme. la Marquise's affairs were freely discussed in the cafés, the clubs and restaurants, and as no one knew the facts of the case, surmises soon became very wild.

On the third day of M. le Marquis's disappearance Papa Mosenstein returned to Paris from Vichy, where he had just completed his annual cure. He arrived at Rue de Grammont at three o'clock in the afternoon, demanded to see Mme. la Marquise at once, and then remained closeted with her in her apartment for over an hour. After which he sent for the inspector of police of the section, with the result that that very same evening M. le Marquis de Firmin-Latour was found locked up in an humble apartment on the top floor of a house in the Rue Daunou, not ten minutes' walk from his own house. When the police—acting on information supplied to them by M. Mauruss Mosenstein—forced their way into that apartment, they were horrified to find M. le Marquis de Firmin-Latour there, tied hand and foot with cords to a chair, his likely calls for help smothered by a woollen shawl wound loosely round the lower part of his face.

He was half dead with inanition, and was conveyed speechless and helpless to his home in the Rue de Grammont, there, presumably, to be nursed back to health by Madame his wife.

5.

Now in all this matter, I ask you, Sir, who ran the greatest risk? Why, I—Hector Ratichon, of course—Hector Ratichon, in whose apartment M. de Firmin-Latour was discovered in a position bordering on absolute inanition. And the proof of this is, that that selfsame night I was arrested at my lodgings at Passy, and charged with robbery and attempted murder.

It was a terrible predicament for a respectable citizen, a man of integrity and reputation, in which to find himself; but Papa Mosenstein was both tenacious and vindictive. His daughter, driven to desperation at last, and terrified that M. le Marquis had indeed been foully murdered by M. de Naquet, had made a clean breast of the whole affair to her father, and he in his turn had put the minions of the law in full possession of all the facts; and since M. le Comte de Naquet had vanished, leaving no manner of trace or clue of his person behind him, the police, needing a victim, fell back on an innocent man. Fortunately, Sir, that innocence clear as crystal soon shines through every calumny. But this was not before I had suffered terrible indignities and all the tortures which base ingratitude can inflict upon a sensitive heart.

Such ingratitude as I am about to relate to you has never been equalled on this earth, and even after all these years, Sir, you see me overcome with emotion at the remembrance of it all. I was under arrest, remember, on a terribly serious charge, but, conscious of mine own innocence and of my unanswerable system of defence, I bore the preliminary examination by the juge d'instruc-tion with exemplary dignity and patience. I knew, you see, that at my very first confrontation with my supposed victim the latter would at once say:

"Ah! but no! This is not the man who assaulted me."

Our plan, which so far had been overwhelmingly successful, had been this.

On the morning of the tenth, M. de Firmin-Latour having pawned the emeralds, and obtained the money for them, was to deposit that money in his own name at the bank of Raynal Frères and then at once go to the office in the Rue Daunou.

There he would be met by Theodore, who would bind him comfortably but securely to a chair, put a shawl around his mouth and finally lock the door on him. Theodore would then go to his mother's and there remain quietly until I needed his services again.

It had been thought inadvisable for me to be seen that morning anywhere in the neighbourhood of the Rue Daunou, but that perfidious reptile Theodore ran no risks in doing what he was told. To begin with he is a past master in the art of worming himself in and out of a house without being seen, and in this case it was his business to exercise a double measure of caution. And secondly, if by some unlucky chance the police did subsequently connect him with the crime, there was I, his employer, a man of integrity and repute, prepared to swear that the man had been in my company at the other end of Paris all the while that M. le Marquis de Firmin-Latour was, by special arrangement, making use of my office in the Rue Daunou, which I had lent him for purposes of business.

Finally it was agreed between us that when M. le Marquis would presently be questioned by the police as to the appearance of the man who had assaulted and robbed him, he would describe him as tall and blond, almost like an Angliche in countenance. Now I possess—as you see, Sir—all the finest characteristics of the Latin race, whilst Theodore looks like nothing on earth, save perhaps a cross between a rat and a monkey.

I wish you to realize, therefore, that no one ran any risks in this affair excepting myself. I, as the proprietor of the apartment where the assault was actually supposed to have taken place, did run a very grave risk, because I could never have proved an alibi. Theodore was such a disreputable mudlark that his testimony on my behalf would have been valueless. But with sublime sacrifice I accepted these risks, and you will presently see, Sir, how I was repaid for my selflessness. I pined in a lonely prison-cell while these two limbs of Satan concocted a plot to rob me of my share in our mutual undertaking.

Well, Sir, the day came when I was taken from my prison-cell for the purpose of being confronted with the man whom I was accused of having assaulted. As you will imagine, I was perfectly calm. According to our plan the confrontation would be the means of setting me free at once. I was conveyed to the house in the Rue de Grammont, and here I was kept waiting for some little time while the juge d'instruction went in to prepare M. le Marquis, who was still far from well. Then I was introduced into the sick-room. I looked about me with the perfect composure of an innocent man about to be vindicated, and calmly gazed on the face of the sick man who was sitting up in his magnificent bed, propped up with pillows.

I met his glance firmly whilst M. le Juge d'instruction placed the question to him in a solemn and earnest tone:

"M. le Marquis de Firmin-Latour, will you look at the prisoner before you and tell us whether you recognize in him the man who assaulted you?"

And that perfidious Marquis, Sir, raised his eyes and looked me squarely— yes! squarely—in the face and said with incredible assurance:

"Yes, Monsieur le Juge, that is the man! I recognize him."

To me it seemed then as if a thunderbolt had crashed through the ceiling and exploded at my feet. I was like one stunned and dazed; the black ingratitude, the abominable treachery, completely deprived me of speech. I felt choked, as if some poisonous effluvia—the poison, Sir, of that man's infamy—had got into my throat. That state of inertia lasted, I believe, less than a second; the next I had uttered a hoarse cry of noble indignation.

"You vampire, you!" I exclaimed. "You viper! You . . ."

I would have thrown myself on him and strangled him with glee, but that the minions of the law had me by the arms and dragged me away out of the hateful presence of that traitor, despite my objurgations and my protestations of innocence. Imagine my feelings when I found myself once more in a prison-cell, my heart filled with unspeakable bitterness against that perfidious Judas. Can you wonder that it took me some time before I could collect my thoughts sufficiently to review my situation, which no doubt to the villain himself who had just played me this abominable trick must have seemed desperate indeed? Ah! I could see it all, of course! He wanted to] see me sent to New Caledonia, whilst he enjoyed the fruits of his unpardonable backsliding. In order to retain the miserable hundred thousand francs which he had promised me he did not hesitate to plunge up to the neck in this heinous conspiracy.

Yes, conspiracy! for the very next day, when I was once more hailed before the juge d'instruction, another confrontation awaited me: this time with that scurvy rogue Theodore. He had been suborned by M. le Marquis to turn against the hand that fed him. What price he was paid for this Judas trick I shall never know, and all that I do know is that he actually swore before the juge d'instruction that M. le Marquis de Firmin-Latour called at my office in the late forenoon of the tenth of October; that I then ordered him—Theodore—to go out to get his dinner first, and then to go all the way over to Neuilly with a message to someone who turned out to be non-existent. He went on to assert that when he returned at six o'clock in the afternoon he found the office door locked, and I—his employer—presumably gone. This at first greatly upset him, because he was supposed to sleep on the premises, but seeing that there was nothing for it but to accept the inevitable, he went round to his mother's rooms at the back of the fish-market and remained there ever since, waiting to hear from me.

That, Sir, was the tissue of lies which that jailbird had concocted for my undoing, knowing well that I could not disprove them because it had been my task on that eventful morning to keep an eye on M. le Marquis whilst he went to the Mont de Piété first, and then to MM. Raynal Frères, the bankers where he deposited the money. For this purpose I had been obliged to don a disguise, which I had not discarded till later in the day, and thus was unable to disprove satisfactorily the monstrous lies told by that perjurer.

Ah! I can see that sympathy for my unmerited misfortunes has filled your eyes with tears. No doubt in your heart you feel that my situation at that hour was indeed desperate, and that I—Hector Ratichon, the confidant of kings, the benefactor of the oppressed—did spend the next few years of my life in a penal settlement, where those arch-malefactors themselves should have been. But no, Sir! Fate may be a fickle jade, rogues may appear triumphant, but not for long, Sir, not for long! It is brains that conquer in the end . . . brains backed by righteousness and by justice.

Whether I had actually foreseen the treachery of those two rattlesnakes, or whether my habitual caution and acumen alone prompted me to take those measures of precaution of which I am about to tell you, I cannot truthfully remember. Certain it is that I did take those precautions which ultimately proved to be the means of compensating me for most that I had suffered.

It had been a part of the original plan that, on the day immediately following the tenth of October, I, in my own capacity as Hector Ratichon, who had been absent from my office for twenty-four hours, would arrive there in the morning, find the place locked, force an entrance into the apartment, and there find M. le Marquis in his pitiable plight. After which I would, of course, immediately notify the police of the mysterious occurrence.

That had been the rôle which I had intended to play. M. le Marquis approved of it and had professed himself quite willing to endure a twenty-four-hours' martyrdom for the sake of half a million francs. But, as I have just had the honour to tell you, something which I will not attempt to explain prompted me at the last moment to modify my plan in one little respect. I thought it too soon to go back to the Rue Daunou within twenty-four hours of our well-contrived coup, and I did not altogether care for the idea of going myself to the police in order to explain to them that I had found a man gagged and bound in my office. The less one has to do with these minions of the law the better. Mind you, I had envisaged the possibility of being accused of assault and robbery, but I did not wish to take, as it were, the very first steps myself in that direction. You might call this a matter of sentiment or of prudence, as you wish.

So I waited until the evening of the second day before I got the key from Theodore. Then before the concierge at 96 Rue Daunou had closed the porte-cochere for the night, I slipped into the house unobserved, ran up the stairs to my office and entered the apartment. I struck a light and made my way to the inner room where the wretched Marquis hung in the chair like a bundle of rags. I called to him, but he made no movement. As I had anticipated, he had fainted for want of food. Of course, I was very sorry for him, for his plight was pitiable, but he was playing for high stakes, and a little starvation does no man any harm. In his case there was half a million at the end of his brief martyrdom, which could, at worst, only last another twenty-four hours. I reckoned that Mme. la Marquise could not keep the secret of her husband's possible whereabouts longer than that, and in any event I was determined that, despite all risks, I would go myself to the police on the following day.

In the meanwhile, since I was here and since M. le Marquis was unconscious, I proceeded then and there to take the precaution which prudence had dictated, and without which, seeing this man's treachery and Theodore's villainy, I should undoubtedly have ended my days as a convict. What I did was to search M. le Marquis's pockets for anything that might subsequently prove useful to me.

I had no definite idea in the matter, you understand; but I had vague notions of finding the bankers' receipt for the half-million francs.

Well, I did not find that, but I did find the receipt from the Mont de Piété for a parure of emeralds on which half a million francs had been lent. This I carefully put away in my waistcoat pocket, but as there was nothing else I wished to do just then I extinguished the light and made my way cautiously out of the apartment and out of the house. No one had seen me enter or go out, and M. le Marquis had not stirred while I went through his pockets.

6.

That, Sir, was the precaution which I had taken in order to safeguard myself against the machinations of traitors. And see how right I was; see how hopeless would have been my plight at this hour when Theodore, too, turned against me like the veritable viper that he was. I never really knew when and under what conditions the infamous bargain was struck which was intended to deprive me of my honour and of my liberty, nor do I know what emolument Theodore was to receive for his treachery. Presumably the two miscreants arranged it all some time during that memorable morning of the tenth even whilst I was risking my life in their service.

As for M. de Firmin-Latour, that worker of iniquity who, in order to save a paltry hundred thousand francs from the hoard which I had helped him to acquire, did not hesitate to commit such an abominable crime, he did not long remain in the enjoyment of his wealth or of his peace of mind.

The very next day I made certain statements before M. le Juge d'instruction with regard to M. Mauruss Mosenstein, which caused the former to summon the worthy Israelite to his bureau, there to be confronted with me. I had nothing more to lose, since those execrable rogues had already, as it were, tightened the rope about my neck, but I had a great deal to gain—revenge above all, and perhaps the gratitude of M. Mosenstein for opening his eyes to the rascality of his son-in-law.

In a stream of eloquent words which could not fail to carry conviction, I gave then and there in the bureau of the juge d'instruction my version of the events of the past few weeks, from the moment when M. le Marquis de Firmin-Latour came to consult me on the subject of his wife's first husband, until the hour when he tried to fasten an abominable crime upon me. I told how I had been deceived by my own employé, Theodore, a man whom I had rescued out of the gutter and loaded with gifts, how by dint of a clever disguise which would have deceived his own mother he had assumed the appearance and personality of M. le Comte de Naquet, first and only lawful lord of the beautiful Rachel Mosenstein. I told of the interviews in my office, my earnest desire to put an end to this abominable blackmailing by informing the police of the whole affair. I told of the false M. de Naquet's threats to create a gigantic scandal which would forever ruin the social position of the so-called Marquis de Firmin-Latour. I told of M. le Marquis's agonized entreaties, his prayers, supplications, that I would do nothing in the matter for the sake of an innocent lady who had already grievously suffered. I spoke of my doubts, my scruples, my desire to do what was just and what was right.

A noble expose of the situation, Sir, you will admit. It left me hot and breathless. I mopped my head with a handkerchief and sank back, gasping, in the arms of the minions of the law. The juge d'instruction ordered my removal, not back to my prison-cell but into his own ante-room, where I presently collapsed upon a very uncomfortable bench and endured the additional humiliation of having a glass of water held to my lips. Water! when I had asked for a drink of wine as my throat felt parched after that lengthy effort at oratory.

However, there I sat and waited patiently whilst, no doubt, M. le Juge d'Instruction and the noble Israelite were comparing notes as to their impression of my marvellous speech. I had not long to wait. Less than ten minutes later I was once more summoned into the presence of M. le Juge; and this time the minions of the law were ordered to remain in the antechamber. I thought this was of good augury; and I waited to hear M. le Juge give forth the order that would at once set me free. But it was M. Mosenstein who first addressed me, and in very truth surprise rendered me momentarily dumb when he did it thus:

"Now then, you consummate rascal, when you have given up the receipt of the Mont de Piété which you stole out of M. le Marquis's pocket you may go and carry on your rogueries elsewhere and call yourself mightily lucky to have escaped so lightly."

I assure you, Sir, that a feather would have knocked me down. The coarse insult, the wanton injustice, had deprived me of the use of my limbs and of my speech. Then the juge d'instruction proceeded dryly:

"Now then, Ratichon, you have heard what M. Mauruss Mosenstein has been good enough to say to you. He did it with my approval and consent. I am prepared to give an *ordonnance de non-lieu* in your favour which will have the effect of at once setting you free if you will restore to this gentleman here the Mont de Piété receipt which you appear to have stolen."

"Sir," I said with consummate dignity in the face of this reiterated taunt, "I have stolen nothing—"

M. le Juge's hand was already on the bell-pull.

"Then," he said coolly, "I can ring for the gendarmes to take you back to the cells, and you will stand your trial for blackmail, theft, assault and robbery."

I put up my hand with an elegant and perfectly calm gesture.

"Your pardon, M. le Juge," I said with the gentle resignation of undeserved martyrdom, "I was about to say that when I re-visited my rooms in the Rue Daunou after a three days' absence, and found the police in possession, I picked up on the floor of my private room a white paper which on subsequent examination proved to be a receipt from the Mont de Piété for some valuable gems, and made out in the name of M. le Marquis de Firmin-Latour."

"What have you done with it, you abominable knave?" the irascible old usurer rejoined roughly, and I regret to say that he grasped his malacca cane with ominous violence.

But I was not to be thus easily intimidated.

"Ah! voilà, M. le Juge," I said with a shrug of the shoulders. "I have mislaid it. I do not know where it is."

"If you do not find it," Mosenstein went on savagely, "you will find yourself on a convict ship before long."

"In which case, no doubt," I retorted with suave urbanity, "the police will search my rooms where I lodge, and they will find the receipt from the Mont de Piété, which I had mislaid. And then the gossip will be all over Paris that Mme. la Marquise de Firmin-Latour had to pawn her jewels in order to satisfy the exigencies of her first and only lawful husband who has since mysteriously disappeared; and some people will vow that he never came back from the Antipodes, whilst others—by far the most numerous—will shrug their shoulders and sigh: 'One never knows!' which will be exceedingly unpleasant for Mme. la Marquise."

Both M. Mauruss Mosenstein and the juge d'instruc-tion said a great deal more that afternoon. I may say that their attitude towards me and the language that they used were positively scandalous. But I had become now the master of the situation and I could afford to ignore their insults. In the end everything was settled quite amicably. I agreed to dispose of the receipt from the Mont de Piété to M. Mauruss Mosenstein for the sum of two hundred francs, and for another hundred I would indicate to him the banking house where his precious son-in-law had deposited the half-million francs obtained for the emeralds. This latter information I would indeed have offered him gratuitously had he but known with what immense pleasure I thus put a spoke in that knavish Marquis's wheel of fortune.

The worthy Israelite further agreed to pay me an annuity of two hundred francs so long as I kept silent upon the entire subject of Mme. la Marquise's first husband and of M. le Marquis's rôle in the mysterious affair of the Rue Daunou. For thus was the affair classed amongst the police records. No one outside the chief actors of the drama and M. le Juge d'Instruction ever knew the true history of how a dashing young cavalry officer came to be assaulted and left to starve for three days in the humble apartment of an attorney-at-law of undisputed repute. And no one outside the private bureau of M. le Juge d'Instruction ever knew what it cost the wealthy M. Mosenstein to have the whole affair "classed" and hushed up.

As for me, I had three hundred francs as payment for work which I had risked my neck and my reputation to accomplish. Three hundred instead of the hundred thousand which I had so richly deserved: that, and a paltry two hundred francs a year, which was to cease the moment that as much as a rumour of the whole affair was breathed in public. As if I could help people talking!

But M. le Marquis did not enjoy the fruits of his villainy, and I had again the satisfaction of seeing him gnaw his finger-nails with rage whenever the lovely Rachel paid for his dinner at fashionable restaurants. Indeed Papa Mosenstein tightened the strings of his money-bags even more securely than he had done in the past. Under threats of prosecution for theft and I know not what, he forced his son-in-law to disgorge that half-million which he had so pleasantly tucked away in the banking house of Raynal Frères, and I was indeed thankful that prudence had, on that memorable morning, suggested to me the advisability of dogging the Marquis's footsteps. I doubt not but what he knew whence had come the thunderbolt which had crushed his last hopes of an independent fortune, and no doubt too he does not cherish feelings of good will towards me.

But this eventuality leaves me cold. He has only himself to thank for his misfortune. Everything would have gone well but for his treachery. We would have become affluent, he and I and Theodore. Theodore has gone to live with his mother, who has a fish-stall in the Halles; she gives him three sous a day for washing down the stall and selling the fish when it has become too odorous for the ordinary customers.

And he might have had five hundred francs for himself and remained my confidential clerk.

CHAPTER IV

CARISSIMO

1.

You must not think for a moment, my dear Sir, that I was ever actually deceived in Theodore. Was it likely that I, who am by temperament and habit accustomed to read human visages like a book, was it likely, I say, that I would fail to see craftiness in those pale, shifty eyes, deceit in the weak, slobbering mouth, intemperance in the whole aspect of the shrunken, slouchy figure which I had, for my subsequent sorrow, so generously rescued from starvation?

Generous? I was more than generous to him. They say that the poor are the friends of the poor, and I told you how poor we were in those days! Ah! but poor! my dear Sir, you have no conception! Meat in Paris in the autumn of 1816 was 24 francs the kilo, and milk 1 franc the quarter litre, not to mention eggs and butter, which were delicacies far beyond the reach of cultured, well-born people like myself.

And yet throughout that trying year I fed Theodore—yes, I fed him. He used to share onion pie with me whenever I partook of it, and he had haricot soup every day, into which I allowed him to boil the skins of all the sausages and the luscious bones of all the cutlets of which I happened to partake. Then think what he cost me in drink! Never could I leave a half or quarter bottle of wine but he would finish it; his impudent fingers made light of every lock and key. I dared not allow as much as a sou to rest in the pocket of my coat but he would ferret it out the moment I hung the coat up in the outer room and my back was turned for a few seconds. After a while I was forced—yes, I, Sir, who have spoken on terms of equality with kings—I was forced to go out and make my own purchases in the neighbouring provision shops. And why? Because if I sent Theodore and gave him a few sous wherewith to make these purchases, he would spend the money at the nearest cabaret in getting drunk on absinthe.

He robbed me, Sir, shamefully, despite the fact that he had ten per cent, commission on all the profits of the firm. I gave him twenty francs out of the money which I had earned at the sweat of my brow in the service of Estelle Bachelier. Twenty francs, Sir! Reckoning two hundred francs as business profit on the affair, a generous provision you will admit! And yet he taunted me with having received a thousand. This was mere guesswork, of course, and I took no notice of his taunts: did the brains that conceived the business deserve no payment? Was my labour to be counted as dross?—the humiliation, the blows which I had to endure while he sat in hoggish content, eating and sleeping without thought for the morrow? After which he calmly pocketed the twenty francs to earn which he had not raised one finger, and then demanded more.

No, no, my dear Sir, you will believe me or not, that man could not go straight. Times out of count he would try and deceive me, despite the fact that, once or twice, he very nearly came hopelessly to grief in the attempt.

Now, just to give you an instance. About this time Paris was in the grip of a gang of dog-thieves as unscrupulous and heartless as they were daring. Can you wonder at it? with that awful penury about and a number of expensive "tou-tous" running about the streets under the very noses of the indigent proletariat? The ladies of the aristocracy and of the wealthy bourgeoisie had imbibed this craze for lap-dogs during their sojourn in England at the time of the emigration, and being women of the Latin race and of undisciplined temperament, they were just then carrying their craze to excess.

As I was saying, this indulgence led to wholesale thieving. Tou-tous were abstracted from their adoring mistresses with marvellous adroitness; whereupon two or three days would elapse while the adoring mistress wept buckets full of tears and set the police of M. Fouché, Duc d'Otrante, by the ears in search of her pet. The next act in the tragi-comedy would be an anonymous demand for money—varying in amount in accordance with the known or supposed wealth of the lady—and an equally anonymous threat of dire vengeance upon the tou-tou if the police were put upon the track of the thieves.

You will ask me, no doubt, what all this had to do with Theodore. Well! I will tell you.

You must know that of late he had become extraordinarily haughty and independent. I could not keep him to his work. His duties were to sweep the office—he did not do it; to light the fires—I had to light them myself every morning; to remain in the anteroom and show clients in—he was never at his post. In fact he was never there when I did want him: morning, noon and night he was out—gadding about and coming home, Sir, only to eat and sleep. I was seriously thinking of giving him the sack. And then one day he disappeared! Yes, Sir, disappeared completely as if the earth had swallowed him up. One morning—it was in the beginning of December and the cold was biting—I arrived at the office and found that his chair-bed which stood in the antechamber had not been slept in; in fact that it had not been made up overnight. In the cupboard I found the remnants of an onion pie, half a sausage, and a quarter of a litre of wine, which proved conclusively that he had not been in to supper.

At first I was not greatly disturbed in my mind. I had found out quite recently that Theodore had some sort of a squalid home of his own somewhere behind the fish-market, together with an old and wholly disreputable mother who plied him with drink whenever he spent an evening with her and either he or she had a franc in their pocket. Still, after these bouts spent in the bosom of his family he usually returned to sleep them off at my expense in my office.

I had unfortunately very little to do that day, so in the late afternoon, not having seen anything of Theodore all day, I turned my steps toward the house behind the fish-market where lived the mother of that ungrateful wretch.

The woman's surprise when I inquired after her precious son was undoubtedly genuine. Her lamentations and crocodile tears certainly were not. She reeked of alcohol, and the one room which she inhabited was indescribably filthy. I offered her half a franc if she gave me authentic news of Theodore, knowing well that for that sum she would have sold him to the devil. But very obviously she knew nothing of his whereabouts, and I soon made haste to shake the dirt of her abode from my heels.

I had become vaguely anxious.

I wondered if he had been murdered somewhere down a back street, and if I should miss him very much.

I did not think that I would.

Moreover, no one could have any object in murdering Theodore. In his own stupid way he was harmless enough, and he certainly was not possessed of anything worth stealing. I myself was not over-fond of the man—but I should not have bothered to murder him.

Still, I was undoubtedly anxious, and slept but little that night thinking of the wretch. When the following morning I arrived at my office and still could see no trace of him, I had serious thoughts of putting the law in motion on his behalf.

Just then, however, an incident occurred which drove all thoughts of such an insignificant personage as Theodore from my mind.

I had just finished tidying up the office when there came a peremptory ring at the outer door, repeated at intervals of twenty seconds or so. It meant giving a hasty glance all round to see that no fragments of onion pie or of cheap claret lingered in unsuspected places, and it meant my going, myself, to open the door to my impatient visitor.

I did it, Sir, and then at the door I stood transfixed. I had seen many beautiful women in my day—great ladies of the Court, brilliant ladies of the Consulate, the Directorate and the Empire—but never in my life had I seen such an exquisite and resplendent apparition as the one which now sailed through the antechamber of my humble abode.

Sir, Hector Ratichon's heart has ever been susceptible to the charms of beauty in distress. This lovely being, Sir, who now at my invitation entered my office and sank with perfect grace into the arm-chair, was in obvious distress. Tears hung on the fringe of her dark lashes, and the gossamer-like handkerchief which she held in her dainty hand was nothing but a wet rag. She gave herself exactly two minutes wherein to compose herself, after which she dried her eyes and turned the full artillery of her bewitching glance upon me.

"Monsieur Ratichon," she began, even before I had taken my accustomed place at my desk and assumed that engaging smile which inspires confidence even in the most timorous; "Monsieur Ratichon, they tell me that you are so clever, and—oh! I am in such trouble."

"Madame," I rejoined with noble simplicity, "you may trust me to do the impossible in order to be of service to you."

Admirably put, you will admit. I have always been counted a master of appropriate diction, and I had been quick enough to note the plain band of gold which encircled the third finger of her dainty left hand, flanked though it was by a multiplicity of diamond, pearl and other jewelled rings.

"You are kind, Monsieur Ratichon," resumed the beauteous creature more calmly. "But indeed you will require all the ingenuity of your resourceful brain in order to help me in this matter. I am struggling in the grip of a relentless fate which, if you do not help me, will leave me broken-hearted."

"Command me, Madame," I riposted quietly.

From out the daintiest of reticules the fair lady now extracted a very greasy and very dirty bit of paper, and handed it to me with the brief request: "Read this, I pray you, my good M. Ratichon." I took the paper. It was a clumsily worded, ill-written, ill-spelt demand for five thousand francs, failing which sum the thing which Madame had lost would forthwith be destroyed.

I looked up, puzzled, at my fair client.

"My darling Carissimo, my dear M. Ratichon," she said in reply to my mute query.

"Carissimo?" I stammered, yet further intrigued.

"My darling pet, a valuable creature, the companion of my lonely hours," she rejoined, once more bursting into tears. "If I lose him, my heart will inevitably break."

I understood at last.

"Madame has lost her dog?" I asked.

She nodded.

"It has been stolen by one of those expert dog thieves, who then levy blackmail on the unfortunate owner?"

Again she nodded in assent.

I read the dirty, almost illegible scrawl through more carefully this time. It was a clumsy notification addressed to Mme. la Comtesse de Nolé de St. Pris to the effect that her tou-tou was for the moment safe, and would be restored to the arms of his fond mistress provided the sum of five thousand francs was deposited in the hands of the bearer of the missive.

Minute directions were then given as to where and how the money was to be deposited. Mme. la Comtesse de Nolé was, on the third day from this at six o'clock in the evening precisely, to go in person and alone to the angle of the Rue Guénégaud and the Rue Mazarine, at the rear of the Institut.

There two men would meet her, one of whom would have Carissimo in his arms; to the other she must hand over the money, whereupon the pet would at once be handed back to her. But if she failed to keep this appointment, or if in the meanwhile she made the slightest attempt to trace the writer of the missive or to lay a trap for his capture by the police, Carissimo would at once meet with a summary death.

These were the usual tactics of experienced dog thieves, only that in this case the demand was certainly exorbitant. Five thousand francs! But even so . . . I cast a rapid and comprehensive glance on the brilliant apparition before me— the jewelled rings, the diamonds in the shell-like ears, the priceless fur coat—and with an expressive shrug of the shoulders I handed the dirty scrap of paper back to its fair recipient.

"Alas, Madame," I said, taking care that she should not guess how much it cost me to give her such advice, "I am afraid that in such cases there is nothing to be done. If you wish to save your pet you will have to pay. . ."

"Ah! but, Monsieur," she exclaimed tearfully, "you don't understand. Carissimo is all the world to me, and this is not the first time, nor yet the second, that he has been stolen from me. Three times, my good M. Ratichon, three times has he been stolen, and three times have I received such peremptory demands for money for his safe return; and every time the demand has been more and more exorbitant. Less than a month ago M. le Comte paid three thousand francs for his recovery."

"Monsieur le Comte?" I queried.

"My husband, Sir," she replied, with an exquisite air of hauteur. "M. le Comte de Nolé de St. Pris."

"Ah, then," I continued calmly, "I fear me that Monsieur de Nolé de St. Pris will have to pay again."

"But he won't!" she now cried out in a voice broken with sobs, and incontinently once more saturated her gossamer handkerchief with her tears.

"Then I see nothing for it, Madame," I rejoined, much against my will with a slight touch of impatience, "I see nothing for it but that yourself . . ."

"Ah! but, Monsieur," she retorted, with a sigh that would have melted a heart of stone, "that is just my difficulty. I cannot pay . . ."

"Madame," I protested.

"Oh! if I had money of my own," she continued, with an adorable gesture of impatience, "I would not worry. Mais voilà: I have not a silver franc of my own to bless myself with. M. le Comte is over generous. He pays all my bills without a murmur—he pays my dressmaker, my furrier; he loads me with gifts and dispenses charity on a lavish scale in my name. I have horses, carriages, servants—everything I can possibly want and more, but I never have more than a few hundred francs to dispose of. Up to now I have never for a moment felt the want of money. To-day, when Carissimo is being lost to me, I feel the entire horror of my position."

"But surely, Madame," I urged, "M. le Comte . . ."

"No, Monsieur," she replied. "M. le Comte has flatly refused this time to pay these abominable thieves for the recovery of Carissimo. He upbraids himself for having yielded to their demands on the three previous occasions. He calls these demands blackmailing, and vows that to give them money again is to encourage them in their nefarious practices. Oh! he has been cruel to me, cruel!—for the first time in my life, Monsieur, my husband has made me unhappy, and if I lose my darling now I shall indeed be broken-hearted."

I was silent for a moment or two. I was beginning to wonder what part I should be expected to play in the tragedy which was being unfolded before me by this lovely and impecunious creature.

"Madame la Comtesse," I suggested tentatively, after a while, "your jewellery . . . you must have a vast number which you seldom wear . . . five thousand francs is soon made up. . . ."

You see, Sir, my hopes of a really good remunerative business had by now dwindled down to vanishing point. All that was left of them was a vague idea that the beautiful Comtesse would perhaps employ me as an intermediary for the sale of some of her jewellery, in which case . . . But already her next words disillusioned me even on that point.

"No, Monsieur," she said; "what would be the use? Through one of the usual perverse tricks of fate, M. le Comte would be sure to inquire after the very piece of jewellery of which I had so disposed, and moreover . . ."

"Moreover—yes, Mme. la Comtesse?"

"Moreover, my husband is right," she concluded decisively. "If I give in to those thieves to-day and pay them five thousand francs, they would only set to work to steal Carissimo again and demand ten thousand francs from me another time."

I was silent. What could I say? Her argument was indeed unanswerable.

"No, my good M. Ratichon," she said very determinedly after a while. "I have quite decided that you must confound those thieves. They have given me three days' grace, as you see in their abominable letter. If after three days the money is not forthcoming, and if in the meanwhile I dare to set a trap for them or in any way communicate with the police, my darling Carissimo will be killed and my heart be broken."

"Madame la Comtesse," I entreated, for of a truth I could not bear to see her cry again.

"You must bring Carissimo back to me, M. Ratichon," she continued peremptorily, "before those awful three days have elapsed."

"I swear that I will," I rejoined solemnly; but I must admit that I did it entirely on the spur of the moment, for of a truth I saw no prospect whatever of being able to accomplish what she desired.

"Without my paying a single louis to those execrable thieves," the exquisite creature went on peremptorily,

"It shall be done, Madame la Comtesse."

"And let me tell you," she now added, with the sweetest and archest of smiles, "that if you succeed in this, M. le Comte de Nolé de St. Pris will gladly pay you the five thousand francs which he refuses to give to those miscreants."

Five thousand francs! A mist swam before my eyes,

"Mais, Madame la Comtesse . . ." I stammered.

"Oh!" she added, with an adorable uptilting of her little chin, "I am not promising what I cannot fulfil. M. le Comte de Nolé only said this morning, apropos of dog thieves, that he would gladly give ten thousand francs to anyone who succeeded in ridding society of such pests."

I could have knelt down on the hard floor, Sir, and . . .

"Well then, Madame," was my ready rejoinder, "why not ten thousand francs to me?"

She bit her coral lips . . . but she also smiled. I could see that my personality and my manners had greatly impressed her.

"I will only be responsible for the first five thousand," she said lightly. "But, for the rest, I can confidently assure you that you will not find a miser in M. le Comte de Nolé de St. Pris."

I could have knelt down on the hard floor, Sir, and kissed her exquisitely shod feet. Five thousand francs certain! Perhaps ten! A fortune, Sir, in those days! One that would keep me in comfort—nay, affluence, until something else turned up. I was swimming in the empyrean and only came rudely to earth when I recollected that I should have to give Theodore something for his share of the business. Ah! fortunately that for the moment he was comfortably out of the way! Thoughts that perhaps he had been murdered after all once more coursed through my brain: not unpleasantly, I'll admit. I would not have raised a finger to hurt the fellow, even though he had treated me with the basest ingratitude and treachery; but if someone else took the trouble to remove him, why indeed should I quarrel with fate?

Back I came swiftly to the happy present. The lovely creature was showing me a beautifully painted miniature of Carissimo, a King Charles spaniel of no common type. This she suggested that I should keep by me for the present for purposes of identification. After this we had to go into the details of the circumstances under which she had lost her pet. She had been for a walk with him, it seems, along the Quai Voltaire, and was returning home by the side of the river, when suddenly a number of workmen in blouses and peaked caps came trooping out of a side street and obstructed her progress. She had Carissimo on the lead, and she at once admitted to me that at first she never thought of connecting this pushing and jostling rabble with any possible theft. She held her ground for awhile, facing the crowd: for a few moments she was right in the midst of it, and just then she felt the dog straining at the lead. She turned round at once with the intention of picking him up, when to her horror she saw that there was only a bundle of something weighty at the end of the lead, and that the dog had disappeared.

The whole incident occurred, the lovely creature declared, within the space of thirty seconds; the next instant the crowd had scattered in several directions, the men running and laughing as they went. Mme. la Comtesse was left standing alone on the quay. Not a passer-by in sight, and the only gendarme visible, a long way down the Quai, had his back turned toward her. Nevertheless she ran and hied him, and presently he turned and, realizing that something was amiss, he too ran to meet her. He listened to her story, swore lustily, but shrugged his shoulders in token that the tale did not surprise him and that but little could be done. Nevertheless he at once summoned those of his colleagues who were on duty in the neighbourhood, and one of them went off immediately to notify the theft at the nearest commissariat of police. After which they all proceeded to a comprehensive scouring of the many tortuous sidestreets of the quartier; but, needless to say, there was no sign of Carissimo or of his abductors.

That night my lovely client went home distracted.

The following evening, when, broken-hearted, she wandered down the quays living over again the agonizing moments during which she lost her pet, a workman in a blue blouse, with a peaked cap pulled well over his eyes, lurched up against her and thrust into her hand the missive which she had just shown me. He then disappeared into the night, and she had only the vaguest possible recollection of his appearance.

That, Sir, was the substance of the story which the lovely creature told me in a voice oft choked with tears. I questioned her very closely and in my most impressive professional manner as to the identity of any one man among the crowd who might have attracted her attention, but all that she could tell me was that she had a vague impression of a wizened hunchback with evil face, shaggy red beard and hair, and a black patch covering the left eye.

2.

Not much data to go on, you will, I think, admit, and I Can assure you, Sir, that had I not possessed that unbounded belief in myself which is the true hall-mark of genius, I would at the outset have felt profoundly discouraged.

As it was, I found just the right words of consolation and of hope wherewith to bow my brilliant client out of my humble apartments, and then to settle down to deep and considered meditation. Nothing, Sir, is so conducive to thought as a long, brisk walk through the crowded streets of Paris. So I brushed my coat, put on my hat at a becoming angle, and started on my way.

I walked as far as Suresnes, and I thought. After that, feeling fatigued, I sat on the terrace of the Café Bourbon, overlooking the river. There I sipped my coffee and thought. I walked back into Paris in the evening, and still thought, and thought, and thought. After that I had some dinner, washed down by an agreeable bottle of wine—did I mention that the lovely creature had given me a hundred francs on account?—then I went for a stroll along the Quai Voltaire, and I may safely say that there is not a single side and tortuous street in its vicinity that I did not explore from end to end during the course of that never to be forgotten evening.

But still my mind remained in a chaotic condition. I had not succeeded in forming any plan. What a quandary, Sir! Oh! what a quandary! Here was I, Hector Ratichon, the confidant of kings, the right hand of two emperors, set to the task of stealing a dog—for that is what I should have to do—from an unscrupulous gang of thieves whose identity, abode and methods were alike unknown to me. Truly, Sir, you will own that this was a herculean task.

Vaguely my thoughts reverted to Theodore. He might have been of good counsel, for he knew more about thieves than I did, but the ungrateful wretch was out of the way on the one occasion when he might have been of use to me who had done so much for him. Indeed, my reason told me that I need not trouble my head about Theodore. He had vanished; that he would come back presently was, of course, an indubitable fact; people like Theodore never vanish completely. He would come back and demand I know not what, his share, perhaps, in a business which was so promising even if it was still so vague.

Five thousand francs! A round sum! If I gave Theodore five hundred the sum would at once appear meagre, unimportant. Four thousand five hundred francs!—it did not even *sound* well to my mind.

So I took care that Theodore vanished from my mental vision as completely as he had done for the last two days from my ken, and as there was nothing more that could be done that evening, I turned my weary footsteps toward my lodgings at Passy.

All that night, Sir, I lay wakeful and tossing in my bed, alternately fuming and rejecting plans for the attainment of that golden goal—the recovery of Mme. de Nolé's pet dog. And the whole of the next day I spent in vain quest. I visited every haunt of ill-fame known to me within the city. I walked about with a pistol in my belt, a hunk of bread and cheese in my pocket, and slowly growing despair in my heart.

In the evening Mme. la Comtesse de Nolé called for news of Carissimo, and I could give her none. She cried, Sir, and implored, and her tears and entreaties got on to my nerves until I felt ready to fall into hysterics. One more day and all my chances of a bright and wealthy future would have vanished. Unless the money was forthcoming on the morrow, the dog would be destroyed, and with him my every hope of that five thousand francs. And though she still irradiated charm and luxury from her entire lovely person, I begged her not to come to the office again, and promised that as soon as I had any news to impart I would at once present myself at her house in the Faubourg St. Germain.

That night I never slept one wink. Think of it, Sir! The next few hours were destined to see me either a prosperous man for many days to come, or a miserable, helpless, disappointed wretch. At eight o'clock I was at my office. Still no news of Theodore. I could now no longer dismiss him from my mind. Something had happened to him, I could have no doubt. This anxiety, added to the other more serious one, drove me to a state bordering on frenzy. I hardly knew what I was doing. I wandered all day up and down the Quai Voltaire, and the Quai des Grands Augustins, and in and around the tortuous streets till I was dog-tired, distracted, half crazy.

I went to the Morgue, thinking to find there Theodore's dead body, and found myself vaguely looking for the mutilated corpse of Carissimo. Indeed, after a while Theodore and Carissimo became so inextricably mixed up in my mind that I could not have told you if I was seeking for the one or for the other and if Mme. la Comtesse de Nolé was now waiting to clasp her pet dog or my man-of-all-work to her exquisite bosom.

She in the meanwhile had received a second, yet more peremptory, missive through the same channel as the previous one. A grimy deformed man, with ginger-coloured hair, and wearing a black patch over one eye, had been seen by one of the servants lolling down the street where Madame lived, and subsequently the concierge discovered that an exceedingly dirty scrap of paper had been thrust under the door of his lodge. The writer of the epistle demanded that Mme. la Comtesse should stand in person at six o'clock that same evening at the corner of the Rue Guénégaud, behind the Institut de France. Two men, each wearing a blue blouse and peaked cap, would meet her there. She must hand over the money to one of them, whilst the other would have Carissimo in his arms. The missive closed with the usual threats that if the police were mixed up in the affair, or the money not forthcoming, Carissimo would be destroyed.

Six o'clock was the hour fixed by these abominable thieves for the final doom of Carissimo. It was now close on five. In a little more than an hour my last hope of five or ten thousand francs and a smile of gratitude from a pair of lovely lips would have gone, never again to return. A great access of righteous rage seized upon me. I determined that those miserable thieves, whoever they were, should suffer for the disappointment which I was now enduring. If I was to lose five thousand francs, they at least should not be left free to pursue their evil ways. I would communicate with the police; the police should meet the miscreants at the corner of the Rue Guénégaud. Carissimo would die; his lovely mistress would be brokenhearted. I would be left to mourn yet another illusion of a possible fortune, but they would suffer in gaol or in New Caledonia the consequences of all their misdeeds.

Fortified by this resolution, I turned my weary footsteps in the direction of the gendarmerie where I intended to lodge my denunciation of those abominable thieves and blackmailers. The night was dark, the streets ill-lighted, the air bitterly cold. A thin drizzle, half rain, half snow, was descending, chilling me to the bone.

I was walking rapidly along the river bank with my coat collar pulled up to my ears, and still instinctively peering up every narrow street which debouches on the quay. Then suddenly I spied Theodore. He was coming down the Rue Beaune, slouching along with head bent in his usual way. He appeared to be carrying something, not exactly heavy, but cumbersome, under his left arm. Within the next few minutes he would have been face to face with me, for I had come to a halt at the angle of the street, determined to have it out with the rascal then and there in spite of the cold and in spite of my anxiety about Carissimo.

All of a sudden he raised his head and saw me, and in a second he turned on his heel and began to run up the street in the direction whence he had come. At once I gave chase. I ran after him—and then, Sir, he came for a second within the circle of light projected by a street lanthorn. But in that one second I had seen that which turned my frozen blood into liquid lava—a tail, Sir!—a dog's tail, fluffy and curly, projecting from beneath that recreant's left arm.

A dog, Sir! a dog! Carissimo! the darling of Mme. la Comtesse de Nolé's heart! Carissimo, the recovery of whom would mean five thousand francs into my pocket! Carissimo! I knew it! For me there existed but one dog in all the world; one dog and one spawn of the devil, one arch-traitor, one limb of Satan! Theodore!

How he had come by Carissimo I had not time to con-conjecture. I called to him. I called his accursed name, using appellations which fell far short of those which he deserved. But the louder I called the faster he ran, and I, breathless, panting, ran after him, determined to run him to earth, fearful lest I should lose him in the darkness of the night. All down the Rue Beaune we ran, and already I could hear behind me the heavy and more leisured tramp of a couple of gendarmes who in their turn had started to give chase.

I tell you, Sir, the sound lent wings to my feet. A chance—a last chance—was being offered me by a benevolent Fate to earn that five thousand francs, the keystone to my future fortune. If I had the strength to seize and hold Theodore until the gendarmes came up, and before he had time to do away with the dog, the five thousand francs could still be mine.

So I ran, Sir, as I had never run before; the beads of perspiration poured down from my forehead; the breath came stertorous and hot from my heaving breast.

Then suddenly Theodore disappeared!

Disappeared, Sir, as if the earth had swallowed him up! A second ago I had seen him dimly, yet distinctly through the veil of snow and rain ahead of me, running with that unmistakable shuffling gait of his, hugging the dog closely under his arm. I had seen him—another effort and I might have touched him!—now the long and deserted street lay dark and mysterious before me, and behind me I could hear the measured tramp of the gendarmes and their peremptory call of "Halt, in the name of the King!"

But not in vain, Sir, am I called Hector Ratichon; not in vain have kings and emperors reposed confidence in my valour and my presence of mind. In less time than it takes to relate I had already marked with my eye the very spot—down the street—where I had last seen Theodore. I hurried forward and saw at once that my surmise had been correct. At that very spot, Sir, there was a low doorway which gave on a dark and dank passage. The door itself was open. I did not hesitate. My life stood in the balance but I did not falter. I might be affronting within the next second or two a gang of desperate thieves, but I did not quake.

I turned into that doorway, Sir; the next moment I felt a stunning blow between my eyes. I just remember calling out with all the strength of my lungs: "Police! Gendarmes! A moi!" Then nothing more.

3.

I woke with the consciousness of violent wordy warfare carried on around me. I was lying on the ground, and the first things I saw were three or four pairs of feet standing close together. Gradually out of the confused hubbub a few sentences struck my reawakened senses.

"The man is drunk."

"I won't have him inside the house."

"I tell you this is a respectable house." This from a shrill feminine voice. "We've never had the law inside our doors before."

By this time I had succeeded in raising myself on my elbow, and, by the dim light of a hanging lamp somewhere down the passage, I was pretty well able to take stock of my surroundings.

The half-dozen bedroom candlesticks on a table up against the wall, the row of keys hanging on hooks fixed to a board above, the glass partition with the words "Concierge" and "Réception" painted across it, all told me that this was one of those small, mostly squalid and disreputable lodging houses or hotels in which this quarter of Paris still abounds.

The two gendarmes who had been running after me were arguing the matter of my presence here with the proprietor of the place and with the concierge.

I struggled to my feet. Whereupon for the space of a solid two minutes I had to bear as calmly as I could the abuse and vituperation which the feminine proprietor of this "respectable house" chose to hurl at my unfortunate head. After which I obtained a hearing from the bewildered minions of the law. To them I gave as brief and succinct a narrative as I could of the events of the past three days. The theft of Carissimo—the disappearance of Theodore—my meeting him a while ago, with the dog under his arm—his second disappearance, this time within the doorway of this "respectable abode," and finally the blow which alone had prevented me from running the abominable thief to earth.

The gendarmes at first were incredulous. I could see that they were still under the belief that my excitement was due to over-indulgence in alcoholic liquor, whilst Madame the proprietress called me an abominable liar for daring to suggest that she harboured thieves within her doors. Then suddenly, as if in vindication of my character, there came from a floor above the sound of a loud, shrill bark.

"Carissimo!" I cried triumphantly. Then I added in a rapid whisper, "Mme. la Comtesse de Nolé is rich. She spoke of a big reward for the recovery of her pet."

These happy words had the effect of stimulating the zeal of the gendarmes. Madame the proprietress grew somewhat confused and incoherent, and finally blurted it out that one of her lodgers—a highly respectable gentleman—did keep a dog, but that there was no crime in that surely.

"One of your lodgers?" queried the representative of the law. "When did he come?"

"About three days ago," she replied sullenly.

"What room does he occupy?"

"Number twenty-five on the third floor."

"He came with his dog?" I interposed quickly, "a spaniel?"

"Yes."

"And your lodger, is he an ugly, slouchy creature—with hooked nose, bleary eyes and shaggy yellow hair?"

But to this she vouchsafed no reply.

Already the matter had passed out of my hands. One of the gendarmes prepared to go upstairs and bade me follow him, whilst he ordered his comrade to remain below and on no account to allow anyone to enter or leave the house. The proprietress and concierge were warned that if they interfered with the due execution of the law they would be severely dealt with; after which we went upstairs.

For a while, as we ascended, we could hear the dog barking furiously, then, presently, just as we reached the upper landing, we heard a loud curse, a scramble, and then a piteous whine quickly smothered.

My very heart stood still. The next moment, however, the gendarme had kicked open the door of No. 25, and I followed him into the room. The place looked dirty and squalid in the extreme—just the sort of place I should have expected Theodore to haunt. It was almost bare save for a table in the centre, a couple of rickety chairs, a broken-down bedstead and an iron stove in the corner. On the table a tallow candle was spluttering and throwing a very feeble circle of light around.

At first glance I thought that the room was empty, then suddenly I heard another violent expletive and became aware of a man sitting close beside the iron stove. He turned to stare at us as we entered, but to my surprise it was not Theodore's ugly face which confronted us. The man sitting there alone in the room where I had expected to see Theodore and Carissimo had a shaggy beard of an undoubted ginger hue. He had on a blue blouse and a peaked cap; beneath his cap his lank hair protruded more decided in colour even than his beard. His head was sunk between his shoulders, and right across his face, from the left eyebrow over the cheek and as far as his ear, he had a hideous crimson scar, which told up vividly against the ghastly pallor of his face.

But there was no sign of Theodore!

At first my friend the gendarme was quite urbane. He asked very politely to see Monsieur's pet dog. Monsieur denied all knowledge of a dog, which denial only tended to establish his own guilt and the veracity of mine own narrative. The gendarme thereupon became more peremptory and the man promptly lost his temper.

I, in the meanwhile, was glancing round the room and soon spied a wall cupboard which had obviously been deliberately screened by the bedstead. While my companion was bringing the whole majesty of the law to bear upon the miscreant's denegations I calmly dragged the bedstead aside and opened the cupboard door.

An ejaculation from my quivering throat brought the gendarme to my side. Crouching in the dark recess of the wall cupboard was Carissimo—not dead, thank goodness! but literally shaking with terror. I pulled him out as gently as I could, for he was so frightened that he growled and snapped viciously at me. I handed him to the gendarme, for by the side of Carissimo I had seen something which literally froze my blood within my veins. It was Theodore's hat and coat, which he had been wearing when I chased him to this house of mystery and of ill-fame, and wrapped together with it was a rag all smeared with blood, whilst the same hideous stains were now distinctly visible on the door of the cupboard itself.

I turned to the gendarme, who at once confronted the abominable malefactor with the obvious proofs of a horrible crime. But the depraved wretch stood by, Sir, perfectly calm and with a cynicism in his whole bearing which I had never before seen equalled!

"I know nothing about that coat," he asserted with a shrug of the shoulders, "nor about the dog."

The gendarme by this time was purple with fury.

"Not know anything about the dog?" he exclaimed in a voice choked with righteous indignation. "Why, he . . . he barked!"

But this indisputable fact in no way disconcerted the miscreant.

"I heard a dog yapping," he said with consummate impudence, "but I thought he was in the next room. No wonder," he added coolly, "since he was in a wall cupboard."

"A wall cupboard," the gendarme rejoined triumphantly, "situated in the very room which you occupy at this moment."

"That is a mistake, my friend," the cynical wretch retorted, undaunted. "I do not occupy this room. I do not lodge in this hotel at all."

"Then how came you to be here?"

"I came on a visit to a friend who happened to be out when I arrived. I found a pleasant fire here, and I sat down to warm myself. Your noisy and unwarranted irruption into this room has so bewildered me that I no longer know whether I am standing on my head or on my heels."

"We'll show you soon enough what you are standing on, my fine fellow," the gendarme riposted with breezy, cheerfulness. "Allons!"

I must say that the pampered minion of the law arose splendidly to the occasion. He seized the miscreant by the arm and took him downstairs, there to confront him with the proprietress of the establishment, while I—with marvellous presence of mind—took possession of Carissimo and hid him as best I could beneath my coat.

In the hall below a surprise and a disappointment were in store for me. I had reached the bottom of the stairs when the shrill feminine accents of Mme. the proprietress struck unpleasantly on my ear.

"No! no! I tell you!" she was saying. "This man is not my lodger. He never came here with a dog. There," she added volubly, and pointing an unwashed finger at Carissimo who was struggling and growling in my arms, "there is the dog. A gentleman brought him with him last Wednesday, when he inquired if he could have a room here for a few nights. Number twenty-five happened to be vacant, and I have no objection to dogs. I let the gentleman have the room, and he paid me twenty sous in advance when he took possession and told me he would keep the room three nights."

"The gentleman? What gentleman?" the gendarme queried, rather inanely I thought.

"My lodger," the woman replied. "He is out for the moment, but he will be back presently I make no doubt. The dog is his. . . ."

"What is he like?" the minion of the law queried abruptly.

"Who? the dog?" she retorted impudently.

"No, no! Your lodger."

Once more the unwashed finger went up and pointed straight at me.

"He described him well enough just now; thin and slouchy in his ways. He has lank, yellow hair, a nose perpetually crimson—with the cold no doubt—and pale, watery eyes. . . ."

"Theodore," I exclaimed mentally.

Bewildered, the gendarme pointed to his prisoner.

"But this man . . . ?" he queried.

"Why," the proprietress replied. "I have seen Monsieur twice, or was it three times? He would visit number twenty-five now and then."

I will not weary you with further accounts of the close examination to which the representative of the law subjected the personnel of the squalid hotel. The concierge and the man of all work did indeed confirm what the proprietress said, and whilst my friend the gendarme —puzzled and floundering—was scratching his head in complete bewilderment, I thought that the opportunity had come for me to slip quietly out by the still open door and make my way as fast as I could to the sumptuous abode in the Faubourg St. Germain, where the gratitude of Mme. de Nolé, together with five thousand francs, were even now awaiting me.

After Madame the proprietress had identified Carissimo, I had once more carefully concealed him under my coat. I was ready to seize my opportunity, after which I would be free to deal with the matter of Theodore's amazing disappearance. Unfortunately just at this moment the little brute gave a yap, and the minion of the law at once interposed and took possession of him.

"The dog belongs to the police now, Sir," he said sternly.

The fatuous jobbernowl wanted his share of the reward, you see.

4.

Having been forced thus to give up Carissimo, and with him all my hopes of a really substantial fortune, I was determined to make the red-polled miscreant suffer for my disappointment, and the minions of the law sweat in the exercise of their duty.

I demanded Theodore! My friend, my comrade, my right hand! I had seen him not ten minutes ago, carrying in his arms this very dog, whom I had subsequently found inside a wall cupboard beside a blood-stained coat. Where was Theodore? Pointing an avenging finger at the red-headed reprobate, I boldly accused him of having murdered my friend with a view to robbing him of the reward offered for the recovery of the dog.

This brought a new train of thought into the wooden pates of the gendarmes. A quartet of them had by this time assembled within the respectable precincts of the Hôtel des Cadets. One of them—senior to the others—at once dispatched a younger comrade to the nearest commissary of police for advice and assistance.

Then he ordered us all into the room pompously labelled "Réception," and there proceeded once more to interrogate us all, making copious notes in his leather-bound book all the time, whilst I, moaning and lamenting the loss of my faithful friend and man of all work, loudly demanded the punishment of his assassin.

Theodore's coat, his hat, the blood-stained rag, had all been brought down from No. 25 and laid out upon the table ready for the inspection of M. the Commissary of Police.

That gentleman arrived with two private agents, armed with full powers and wrapped in the magnificent imperturbability of the law. The gendarme had already put him *au fait* of the events, and as soon as he was seated behind the table upon which reposed the "pièces de conviction," he in his turn proceeded to interrogate the ginger-pated miscreant.

But strive how he might, M. the Commissary elicited no further information from him than that which we all already possessed. The man gave his name as Aristide Nicolet. He had no fixed abode. He had come to visit his friend who lodged in No. 25 in the Hôtel des Cadets. Not finding him at home he had sat by the fire and had waited for him. He knew absolutely nothing of the dog and absolutely nothing of the whereabouts of Theodore.

"We'll soon see about that!" asserted M. the Commissary.

He ordered a perquisition of every room and every corner of the hotel, Madame the proprietress loudly lamenting that she and her respectable house would henceforth be disgraced for ever. But the thieves—whoever they were— were clever. Not a trace of any illicit practice was found on the premises—and not a trace of Theodore.

Had he indeed been murdered? The thought now had taken root in my mind. For the moment I had even forgotten Carissimo and my vanished five thousand francs.

Well, Sir! Aristide Nicolet was marched off to the depot—still protesting his innocence. The next day he was confronted with Mme. la Comtesse de Nolé, who could not say more than that he might have formed part of the gang who had jostled her on the Quai Voltaire, whilst the servant who had taken the missive from him failed to recognize him.

Carissimo was restored to the arms of his loving mistress, but the reward for his recovery had to be shared between the police and myself: three thousand francs going to the police who apprehended the thief, and two thousand to me who had put them on the track.

It was not a fortune, Sir, but I had to be satisfied. But in the meanwhile the disappearance of Theodore had remained an unfathomable mystery. No amount of questionings and cross-questionings, no amount of confrontations and perquisitions, had brought any new matter to light. Aristide Nicolet persisted in his statements, as did the proprietress and the concierge of the Hôtel des Cadets in theirs. Theodore had undoubtedly occupied room No. 25 in the hotel during the three days while I was racking my brain as to what had become of him. I equally undoubtedly saw him for a few moments running up the Rue Beaune with Carissimo's tail projecting beneath his coat. Then he entered the open doorway of the hotel, and henceforth his whereabouts remained a baffling mystery.

Beyond his coat and hat, the stained rag and the dog himself, there was not the faintest indication of what became of him after that. The concierge vowed that he did not enter the hotel—Aristide Nicolet vowed that he did not enter No. 25. But then the dog was in the cupboard, and so were the hat and coat; and even the police were bound to admit that in the short space of time between my last glimpse of Theodore and the gendarme's entry into room 25 it would be impossible for the most experienced criminal on earth to murder a man, conceal every trace of the crime, and so to dispose of the body as to baffle the most minute inquiry and the most exhaustive search.

Sometimes when I thought the whole matter out I felt that I was growing crazy.

5.

Thus about a week or ten days went by and I had just come reluctantly to the conclusion that there must be some truth in the old mediaeval legends which tell us that the devil runs away with his elect from time to time, when I received a summons from M. the Commissary of Police to present myself at his bureau.

He was pleasant and urbane as usual, but to my anxious query after Theodore he only gave me the old reply: "No trace of him can be found."

Then he added: "We must therefore take it for granted, my good M. Ratichon, that your man of all work is—of his own free will—keeping out of the way. The murder theory is untenable; we have had to abandon it. The total disappearance of the body is an unanswerable argument against it. Would you care to offer a reward for information leading to the recovery of your missing friend?"

I hesitated. I certainly was not prepared to pay anyone for finding Theodore.

"Think it over, my good M. Ratichon," rejoined M. le Commissaire pleasantly. "But in the meanwhile I must tell you that we have decided to set Aristide Nicolet free. There is not a particle of evidence against him either in the matter of the dog or of that of your friend. Mme. de Nolé's servants cannot swear to his identity, whilst you have sworn that you last saw the dog in your man's arms. That being so, I feel that we have no right to detain an innocent man."

Well, Sir, what could I say? I knew well enough that there was not a tittle of solid evidence against the man Nicolet, nor had I the power to move the police of His Majesty the King from their decision. In my heart of hearts I had the firm conviction that the ginger-polled ruffian knew all about Carissimo and all about the present whereabouts of that rascal Theodore. But what could I say, Sir? What could I do?

I went home that night to my lodgings at Passy more perplexed than ever I had been in my life before.

The next morning I arrived at my office soon after nine. The problem had presented itself to me during the night of finding a new man of all work who would serve me on the same terms as that ungrateful wretch Theodore.

I mounted the stairs with a heavy step and opened the outer door of my apartment with my private key; and then, Sir, I assure you that for one brief moment I felt that my knees were giving way under me and that I should presently measure my full length on the floor.

There, sitting at the table in my private room, was Theodore. He had donned one of the many suits of clothes which I always kept at the office for purposes of my business, and he was calmly consuming a luscious sausage which was to have been part of my dinner today, and finishing a half-bottle of my best Bordeaux.

He appeared wholly unconscious of his enormities, and when I taxed him with his villainies and plied him with peremptory questions he met me with a dogged silence and a sulky attitude which I have never seen equalled in all my life. He flatly denied that he had ever walked the streets of Paris with a dog under his arm, or that I had ever chased him up the Rue Beaune. He denied ever having lodged in the Hôtel des Cadets, or been acquainted with its proprietress, or with a red-polled, hunchback miscreant named Aristide Nicolet. He denied that the coat and hat found in room No. 25 were his; in fact, he denied everything, and with an impudence, Sir, which was past belief.

But he put the crown to his insolence when he finally demanded two hundred francs from me: his share in the sum paid to me by Mme. de Nolé for the recovery of her dog. He demanded this, Sir, in the name of justice and of equity, and even brandished our partnership contract in my face.

I was so irate at his audacity, so disgusted that presently I felt that I could not bear the sight of him any longer. I turned my back on him and walked out of my own private room, leaving him there still munching my sausage and drinking my Bordeaux.

I was going through the antechamber with a view to going out into the street for a little fresh air when something in the aspect of the chair-bedstead on which that abominable brute Theodore had apparently spent the night attracted my attention. I turned over one of the cushions, and with a cry of rage which I took no pains to suppress I seized upon what I found lying beneath: a blue linen blouse, Sir, a peaked cap, a ginger-coloured wig and beard!

The villain! The abominable mountebank! The wretch! The . . . I was wellnigh choking with wrath.

With the damning pieces of conviction in my hand, I rushed back into the inner room. Already my cry of indignation had aroused the vampire from his orgy. He stood before me sheepish, grinning, and taunted me, Sir—taunted me for my blindness in not recognizing him under the disguise of the so-called Aristide Nicolet.

It was a disguise which he had kept by him in case of an emergency when first he decided to start business as a dog thief. Carissimo had been his first serious venture and but for my interference it would have been a wholly successful one. He had worked the whole thing out with marvellous cleverness, being greatly assisted by Madame Sand, the proprietress of the Hôtel des Cadets, who was a friend of his mother's. The lady, it seems, carried on a lucrative business of the same sort herself, and she undertook to furnish him with the necessary confederates for the carrying out of his plan. The proceeds of the affair were to be shared equally between himself and Madame; the confederates, who helped to jostle Mme. de Nolé whilst her dog was being stolen, were to receive five francs each for their trouble.

When he met me at the corner of the Rue Beaune he was on his way to the Rue Guénégaud, hoping to exchange Carissimo for five thousand francs. When he met me, however, he felt that the best thing to do for the moment was to seek safety in flight. He had only just time to run back to the hotel to warn Mme. Sand of my approach and beg her to detain me at any cost. Then he flew up the stairs, changed into his disguise, Carissimo barking all the time furiously. Whilst he was trying to pacify the dog, the latter bit him severely in the arm, drawing a good deal of blood—the crimson scar across his face was a last happy inspiration which put the finishing touch to his disguise and to the hoodwinking of the police and of me. He had only just time to staunch the blood from his arm and to thrust his own clothes and Carissimo into the wall cupboard when the gendarme and I burst in upon him.

I could only gasp. For one brief moment the thought rushed through my mind that I would denounce him to the police for . . . for . . .

But that was just the trouble. Of what could I accuse him? Of murdering himself or of stealing Mme. de Nolé's dog? The commissary would hardly listen to such a tale . . . and it would make me seem ridiculous. . . .

So I gave Theodore the soundest thrashing he ever had in his life, and fifty francs to keep his mouth shut.

But did I not tell you that he was a monster of ingratitude?

CHAPTER V

THE TOYS

1.

You are right, Sir, I very seldom speak of my halcyon days—those days when the greatest monarch the world has ever known honoured me with his intimacy and confidence. I had my office in the Rue St. Roch then, at the top of a house just by the church, and not a stone's throw from the palace, and I can tell you, Sir, that in those days ministers of state, foreign ambassadors, aye! and members of His Majesty's household, were up and down my staircase at all hours of the day. I had not yet met Theodore then, and fate was wont to smile on me.

As for M. le Duc d'Otrante, Minister of Police, he would send to me or for me whenever an intricate case required special acumen, resourcefulness and secrecy. Thus in the matter of the English files—have I told you of it before? No? Well, then, you shall hear.

Those were the days, Sir, when the Emperor's Berlin Decrees were going to sweep the world clear of English commerce and of English enterprise. It was not a case of paying heavy duty on English goods, or a still heavier fine if you smuggled; it was total prohibition, and hanging if you were caught bringing so much as a metre of Bradford cloth or half a dozen Sheffield files into the country. But you know how it is, Sir: the more strict the law the more ready are certain lawless human creatures to break it. Never was smuggling so rife as it was in those days—I am speaking now of 1810 or 11—never was it so daring or smugglers so reckless.

M. le Duc d'Otrante had his hands full, I can tell you. It had become a matter for the secret police; the coastguard or customs officials were no longer able to deal with it.

Then one day Hypolite Leroux came to see me. I knew the man well—a keen sleuthhound if ever there was one—and well did he deserve his name, for he was as red as a fox.

"Ratichon," he said to me, without preamble, as soon as he had seated himself opposite to me, and I had placed half a bottle of good Bordeaux and a couple of glasses on the table. "I want your help in the matter of these English files. We have done all that we can in our department. M. le Duc has doubled the customs personnel on the Swiss frontier, the coastguard is both keen and efficient, and yet we know that at the present moment there are thousands of English files used in this country, even inside His Majesty's own armament works. M. le Duc d'Otrante is determined to put an end to the scandal. He has offered a big reward for information which will lead to the conviction of one or more of the chief culprits, and I am determined to get that reward—with your help, if you will give it."

"What is the reward?" I asked simply.

"Five thousand francs," he replied. "Your knowledge of English and Italian is what caused me to offer you a share in this splendid enterprise—"

"It's no good lying to me, Leroux," I broke in quietly, "if we are going to work amicably together."

He swore.

"The reward is ten thousand francs." I made the shot at a venture, knowing my man well.

"I swear that it is not," he asserted hotly.

"Swear again," I retorted, "for I'll not deal with you for less than five thousand."

He did swear again and protested loudly. But I was firm.

"Have another glass of wine," I said.

After which he gave in.

The affair was bound to be risky. Smugglers of English goods were determined and desperate men who were playing for high stakes and risking their necks on the board. In all matters of smuggling a knowledge of foreign languages was an invaluable asset. I spoke Italian well and knew some English. I knew my worth. We both drank a glass of cognac and sealed our bond then and there.

After which Leroux drew his chair closer to my desk.

"Listen, then," he said. "You know the firm of Fournier Frères, in the Rue Colbert?"

"By name, of course. Cutlers and surgical instrument makers by appointment to His Majesty. What about them?"

"M. le Duc has had his eyes on them for some time."

"Fournier Frères!" I ejaculated. "Impossible! A more reputable firm does not exist in France."

"I know, I know," he rejoined impatiently. "And yet it is a curious fact that M. Aristide Fournier, the junior partner, has lately bought for himself a house at St. Claude."

"At St. Claude?" I ejaculated.

"Yes," he responded dryly. "Very near to Gex, what?"

I shrugged my shoulders, for indeed the circumstances did appear somewhat strange.

Do you know Gex, my dear Sir? Ah, it is a curious and romantic spot. It has possibilities, both natural and political, which appear to have been expressly devised for the benefit of the smuggling fraternity. Nestling in the midst of the Jura mountains, it is outside the customs zone of the Empire. So you see the possibilities, do you not? Gex soon became the picturesque warehouse of every conceivable kind of contraband goods. On one side of it there was the Swiss frontier, and the Swiss Government was always willing to close one eye in the matter of customs provided its palm was sufficiently greased by the light-fingered gentry. No difficulty, therefore, as you see, in getting contraband goods—even English ones—as far as Gex.

Here they could be kept hidden until a fitting opportunity occurred for smuggling them into France, opportunities for which the Jura, with their narrow defiles and difficult mountain paths, afforded magnificent scope. St. Claude, of which Leroux had just spoken as the place where M. Aristide Fournier had recently bought himself a house, is in France, only a few kilometres from the neutral zone of Gex. It seemed a strange spot to choose for a wealthy and fashionable member of Parisian bourgeois society, I was bound to admit.

"But," I mused, "one cannot go to Gex without a permit from the police."

"Not by road," Leroux assented. "But you will own that there are means available to men who are young and vigorous like M. Fournier, who moreover, I understand, is an accomplished mountaineer. You know Gex, of course?"

I had crossed the Jura once, in my youth, but was not very intimately familiar with the district. Leroux had a carefully drawn-out map of it in his pocket; this he laid out before me.

"These two roads," he began, tracing the windings of a couple of thin red lines on the map with the point of his finger, "are the only two made ones that lead in and out of the district. Here is the Valserine," he went on, pointing to a blue line, "which flows from north to south, and both the roads wind over bridges that span the river close to our frontier. The French customs stations are on our side of those bridges. But, besides those two roads, the frontier can, of course, be crossed by one or other of the innumerable mountain tracks which are only accessible to pedestrians or mules. That is where our customs officials are powerless, for the tracks are precipitous and offer unlimited cover to those who know every inch of the ground. Several of them lead directly into St. Claude, at some considerable distance from the customs stations, and it is these tracks which are being used by M. Aristide Fournier for the felonious purpose of trading with the enemy—on this I would stake my life. But I mean to be even with him, and if I get the help which I require from you, I am convinced that I can lay him by the heels."

"I am your man," I concluded simply.

"Very well," he resumed. "Are you prepared to journey with me to Gex?"

"When do you start?"

"To-day."

"I shall be ready."

He gave a deep sigh of satisfaction.

"Then listen to my plan," he said. "We'll journey together as far as St. Claude; from there you will push on to Gex, and take up your abode in the city, styling yourself an interpreter. This will give you the opportunity of mixing with some of the smuggling fraternity, and it will be your duty to keep both your eyes and ears open. I, on the other hand, will take up my quarters at Mijoux, the French customs station, which is on the frontier, about half a dozen kilometres from Gex. Every day I'll arrange to meet you, either at the latter place or somewhere half-way, and hear what news you may have to tell me. And mind, Ratichon," he added sternly, "it means running straight, or the reward will slip through our fingers."

I chose to ignore the coarse insinuation, and only riposted quietly:

"I must have money on account. I am a poor man, and will be out of pocket by the transaction from the hour I start for Gex to that when you pay me my fair share of the reward."

By way of a reply he took out a case from his pocket. I saw that it was bulging over with banknotes, which confirmed me in my conviction both that he was actually an emissary of the Minister of Police and that I could have demanded an additional thousand francs without fear of losing the business.

"I'll give you five hundred on account," he said as he licked his ugly thumb preparatory to counting out the money before me.

"Make it a thousand," I retorted; "and call it 'additional,' not 'on account.'"

He tried to argue.

"I am not keen on the business," I said with calm dignity, "so if you think that I am asking too much—there are others, no doubt, who would do the work for less."

It was a bold move. But it succeeded. Leroux laughed and shrugged his shoulders. Then he counted out ten hundred-franc notes and laid them out upon the desk. But before I could touch them he laid his large bony hands over the lot and, looking me straight between the eyes, he said with earnest significance:

"English files are worth as much as twenty francs apiece in the market."

"I know."

"Fournier Frères would not take the risks which they are doing for a consignment of less than ten thousand."

"I doubt if they would," I rejoined blandly.

"It will be your business to find out how and when the smugglers propose to get their next consignment over the frontier."

"Exactly."

"And to communicate any information you may have obtained to me."

"And to keep an eye on the valuable cargo, of course?" I concluded.

"Yes," he said roughly, "an eye. But hands off, understand, my good Ratichon, or there'll be trouble."

He did not wait to hear my indignant protest. He had risen to his feet, and had already turned to go. Now he stretched his great coarse hand out to me.

"All in good part, eh?"

I took his hand. He meant no harm, did old Leroux. He was just a common, vulgar fellow who did not know a gentleman when he saw one.

And we parted the best of friends.

2.

A week later I was at Gex. At St. Claude I had parted from Leroux, and then hired a chaise to take me to my destination. It was a matter of fifteen kilometres by road over the frontier of the customs zone and through the most superb scenery I had ever seen in my life. We drove through narrow gorges, on each side of which the mountain heights rose rugged and precipitous to incalculable altitudes above. From time to time only did I get peeps of almost imperceptible tracks along the declivities, tracks on which it seemed as if goats alone could obtain a footing. Once—hundreds of feet above me—I spied a couple of mules descending what seemed like a sheer perpendicular path down the mountain side. The animals appeared to be heavily laden, and I marvelled what forbidden goods lay hidden within their packs and whether in the days that were to come I too should be called upon to risk my life on those declivities following in the footsteps of the reckless and desperate criminals whom it was my duty to pursue.

I confess that at the thought, and with those pictures of grim nature before me, I felt an unpleasant shiver coursing down my spine.

Nothing of importance occurred during the first fortnight of my sojourn at Gex. I was installed in moderately comfortable, furnished rooms in the heart of the city, close to the church and market square. In one of my front windows, situated on the ground floor, I had placed a card bearing the inscription: "Aristide Barrot, Interpreter," and below, "Anglais, Allemand, Italien." I had even had a few clients—conversations between the local police and some poor wretches caught in the act of smuggling a few yards of Swiss silk or a couple of cream cheeses over the French frontier, and sent back to Gex to be dealt with by the local authorities.

Leroux had found lodgings at Mijoux, and twice daily he walked over to Gex to consult with me. We met, mornings and evenings, at the café restaurant of the Crâne Chauve, an obscure little tavern situated on the outskirts of the city. He was waxing impatient at what he called my supineness, for indeed so far I had had nothing to report.

There was no sign of M. Aristide Fournier. No one in Gex appeared to know anything about him, though the proprietor of the principal hotel in the town did recollect having had a visitor of that name once or twice during the past year. But, of course, during this early stage of my stay in the town it was impossible for me to believe anything that I was told. I had not yet succeeded in winning the confidence of the inhabitants, and it was soon pretty evident to me that the whole countryside was engaged in the perilous industry of smuggling. Everyone from the mayor downwards did a bit of a deal now and again in contraband goods. In ordinary cases it only meant fines if one was caught, or perhaps imprisonment for repeated offenses.

But four or five days after my arrival at Gex I saw three fellows handed over to the police of the department. They had been caught in the act of trying to ford the Valserine with half a dozen pack-mules laden with English cloth. They were hanged at St. Claude two days later.

I can assure you, Sir, that the news of this summary administration of justice sent another cold shiver down my spine, and I marvelled if indeed Leroux's surmises were correct and if a respectable tradesman like Aristide Fournier would take such terrible risks even for the sake of heavy gains.

I had been in Gex just a fortnight when the weather, which hitherto had been splendid, turned to squalls and storms. We were then in the second week of September. A torrential rain had fallen the whole of one day, during which I had only been out in order to meet Leroux, as usual, at the Café du Crâne Chauve. I had just come home from our evening meeting—it was then ten o'clock—and I was preparing to go comfortably to bed, when I was startled by a violent ring at the front-door bell.

I had only just time to wonder if this belated visitor desired to see me or my worthy landlady, Mme. Bournon, when her heavy footsteps resounded along the passage. The next moment I heard my name spoken peremptorily by a harsh voice, and Mme. Bournon's reply that M. Aristide Barrot was indeed within. A few seconds later she ushered my nocturnal visitor into my room.

He was wrapped in a dark mantle from head to foot, and he wore a wide-brimmed hat pulled right over his eyes. He did not remove either as he addressed me without further preamble.

"You are an interpreter, Sir?" he queried, speaking very rapidly and in sharp commanding tones.

"At your service," I replied.

"My name is Ernest Berty. I want you to come with me at once to my house. I require your services as intermediary between myself and some men who have come to see me on business. These men whom I wish you to see are Russians," he added, I fancied as an afterthought, "but they speak English fluently."

I suppose that I looked just as I felt—somewhat dubious owing to the lateness of the hour and the darkness of the night, not to speak of the abominable weather, for he continued with marked impatience:

"It is imperative that you should come at once. Though my house is at some little distance from here, I have a chaise outside which will also bring you back, and," he added significantly, "I will pay you whatever you demand."

"It is very late," I demurred, "the weather—"

"Your fee, man!" he broke in roughly, "and let's get on!"

"Five hundred francs," I said at a venture.

"Come!" was his curt reply. "I will give you the money as we drive along."

I wished I had made it a thousand; apparently my services were worth a great deal to him. However, I picked up my mantle and my hat, and within a few seconds was ready to go. I shouted up to Mme. Bournon that I would not be home for a couple of hours, but that as I had my key I need not disturb her when I returned.

Once outside the door I almost regretted my ready acquiescence in this nocturnal adventure. The rain was beating down unmercifully, and at first I saw no sign of a vehicle; but in answer to my visitor's sharp command I followed him down the street as far as the market square, at the corner of which I spied the dim outline of a carriage and a couple of horses.

Without wasting too many words, M. Ernest Berty bundled me into the carriage, and very soon we were on the way. The night was impenetrably dark and the chaise more than ordinarily rickety. I had but little opportunity to ascertain which way we were going. A small lanthorn fixed opposite to me in the interior of the carriage, and flickering incessantly before my eyes, made it still more impossible for me to see anything outside the narrow window. My companion sat beside me, silent and absorbed. After a while I ventured to ask him which way we were driving.

"Through the town," he replied curtly. "My house is just outside Divonne."

Now, Divonne is, as I knew, quite close to the Swiss frontier. It is a matter of seven or eight kilometres—an hour's drive at the very least in this supremely uncomfortable vehicle. I tried to induce further conversation, but made no headway against my companion's taciturnity. However, I had little cause for complaint in another direction. After the first quarter of an hour, and when we had left the cobblestones of the city behind us, he drew a bundle of notes from his pocket, and by the flickering light of the lanthorn he counted out ten fifty-franc notes and handed them without another word to me.

The drive was unspeakably wearisome; but after a while I suppose that the monotonous rumbling of the wheels and the incessant patter of the rain against the window-panes lulled me into a kind of torpor. Certain it is that presently— much sooner than I had anticipated—the chaise drew up with a jerk, and I was roused to full consciousness by hearing M. Berty's voice saying curtly:

"Here we are! Come with me!"

I was stiff, Sir, and I was shivering—not so much with cold as with excitement. You will readily understand that all my faculties were now on the qui vive. Somehow or other during the wearisome drive by the side of my close-tongued companion my mind had fastened on the certitude that my adventure of this night bore a close connexion to the firm of Fournier Frères and to the English files which were causing so many sleepless nights to M. le Duc d'Otrante, Minister of Police.

But nothing in my manner, as I stepped out of the carriage under the porch of the house which loomed dark and massive out of the surrounding gloom, betrayed anything of what I felt. Outwardly I was just a worthy bourgeois, an interpreter by profession, and delighted at the remunerative work so opportunely put in my way.

The house itself appeared lonely as well as dark. M. Berty led the way across a narrow passage, at the end of which there was a door which he pushed open, saying in his usual abrupt manner: "Go in there and wait. I'll send for you directly."

Then he closed the door on me, and I heard his footsteps recrossing the corridor and presently ascending some stairs. I was left alone in a small, sparsely furnished room, dimly lighted by an oil lamp which hung down from the ceiling.

There was a table in the middle of the room, a square of carpet on the floor, and a couple of chairs beside a small iron stove. I noticed that the single window was closely shuttered and barred. I sat down and waited. At first the silence around me was only broken by the pattering of the rain against the shutters and the soughing of the wind down the iron chimney pipe, but after a little while my senses, which by this time had become super-acute, were conscious of various noises within the house itself: footsteps overhead, a confused murmur of voices, and anon the unmistakable sound of a female voice raised as if in entreaty or in complaint.

Somehow a vague feeling of alarm possessed itself of my nervous system. I began to realise my position—alone, a stranger in a house as to whose situation I had not the remotest idea, and among a set of men who, if my surmises were correct, were nothing less than a gang of determined and dangerous criminals. The voices, especially the female one, were now sounding more clear. I tiptoed to the door, and very gently opened it. There was indeed no mistaking the tone of desperate pleading which came from some room above and through & woman's lips. I even caught the words: "Oh, don't! Oh, don't! Not again!" repeated at intervals with pitiable insistence.

Mastering my not unnatural anxiety, I opened the door a little farther and slipped out into the passage, all my instincts of chivalry towards beauty in distress aroused by those piteous cries. Forgetful of every possible danger and of all prudence, I had already darted down the corridor, determined to do my duty as a gentleman as soon as I had ascertained whence had come those cries of anguish, when I heard the frou-frou of skirts and a rapid patter of small feet down the stairs. The next moment a radiant vision, all white muslin, fair curls and the scent of violets, descended on me from above, a soft hand closed over mine and drew me, unresisting, back into the room from whence I had just come.

Bewildered, I gazed on the winsome apparition before me, and beheld a young girl, slender as a lily, dressed in a soft, clinging gown which made her appear more slender still, her fair hair arranged in a tangle of unruly curls round the dainty oval of her face.

She was exquisite, Sir! And the slenderness of her! You cannot imagine it! She looked like a young sapling bending to the gale. But what cut me to the heart was the look of terror and of misery in her face. She clasped her hands together and the tears gathered in her eyes.

"Go, Sir, go at once!" she murmured under her breath, speaking very rapidly. "Do not waste a minute, I beg of you! As you value your life, go before it is too late!"

"But, Mademoiselle," I stammered; for indeed her words and appearance had roused all my worst fears, but also all my instincts of the sleuth-hound scenting his quarry.

"Don't argue, I beg of you," continued the lovely creature, who indeed seemed the prey of overwhelming emotions—fear, horror, pity. "When he comes back do not let him find you here. I'll explain, I'll know what to say, only I entreat you—go!"

Sir, I have many faults, but cowardice does not happen to be one of them, and the more the angel pleaded the more determined was I to see this business through. I was, of course, quite convinced by now that I was on the track of M. Aristide Fournier and the English files, and I was not going to let five thousand francs and the gratitude of the Minister of Police slip through my fingers so easily.

"Mademoiselle," I rejoined as calmly as I could, "let me assure you that though your anxiety for me is like manna to a starving man, I have no fears for my own safety. I have come here in the capacity of a humble interpreter; I certainly am not worth putting out of the way. Moreover, I have been paid for my services, and these I will render to my employer to the best of my capabilities."

"Ah, but you don't know," she retorted, not departing one jot from her attitude of terror and of entreaty, "you don't understand. This house, Monsieur," she added in a hoarse whisper, "is nothing but a den of criminals wherein no honest man or woman is safe."

"Pardon, Mademoiselle," I riposted as lightly and as gallantly as I could, "I see before me the living proof that angels, at any rate, dwell therein."

"Alas! Sir," she rejoined, with a heart-rending sigh, "if you mean me, I am only to be pitied. My dear mother and I are naught but slaves to the will of my brother, who uses us as tools for his nefarious ends."

"But . . ." I stammered, horrified beyond speech at the vista of villainy which her words had opened up before me.

"My mother, Sir," she said simply, "is old and ailing; she is dying of anguish at sight of her son's misdeeds. I would not, could not leave her, yet I would give my life to see her free from that miscreant's clutches!"

My whole soul was stirred to its depths by the intensity of passion which rang through this delicate creature's words. What weird and awesome mystery of iniquity and of crime lay hid, I wondered, between these walls? In what tragedy had I thus accidentally become involved while fulfilling my prosaic duty in the interest of His Majesty's exchequer? As in a flash it suddenly came to me that perhaps I could serve both this lovely creature and the Emperor better by going out of the house now, and lying hidden all the night through somewhere in its vicinity until in daylight I could locate its exact situation. Then I could communicate with Leroux at once and procure the apprehension of this Berty— or Fournier—who apparently was a desperate criminal. Already a bold plan was taking shape in my brain, and with my mind's eye I had measured the distance which separated me from the front door and safety when, in the distance, I heard heavy footsteps slowly descending the stairs. I looked at my lovely companion, and saw her eyes gradually dilating with increased horror. She gave a smothered cry, pressed her handkerchief to her lips, then she murmured hoarsely, "Too late!" and fled precipitately from the room, leaving me a prey to mingled emotions such as I had never experienced before.

3.

A moment or two later M. Ernest Berty, or whatever his real name may have been, entered the room. Whether he had encountered his exquisite sister on the corridor or the stairs, I could not tell; his face, in the dim light of the hanging lamp, looked impenetrable and sinister.

"This way, M. Barrot," he said curtly.

Just for one brief moment the thought occurred to me to throw myself upon him with my whole weight—which was considerable—and make a wild dash for the front door. But it was more than probable that I should be intercepted and brought back, after which no doubt I would be an object of suspicion to these rascals and my life would not be worth an hour's purchase. With the young girl's warnings ringing in my ears, I felt that my one chance of safety and of circumventing these criminals lay in my seeming ingenuousness and complete guileless-ness.

I assumed a perfect professional manner and followed my companion up the stairs. He ushered me into a room just above the one where I had been waiting up to now. Three men dressed in rough clothes were sitting at a table on which stood a couple of tankards and four empty pewter mugs. My employer offered me a glass of ale, which I declined. Then we got to work.

At the first words which M. Berty uttered I knew that all my surmises had been correct. Whether he himself was M. Aristide Fournier, or another partner of that firm, or some other rascal engaged in nefarious doings, I could not know; certain it was that through the medium of cipher words and phrases which he thought were unintelligible to me, and which he ordered me to interpret into English, he was giving directions to the three men with regard to the convoying of contraband cargo over the frontier.

There was much talk of "toys" and "babies"—the latter were to take a walk in the mountains and to avoid the "thorns"; the "toys" were to be securely fastened and well protected against water. It was obviously a case of mules and of the goods, the "thorns" being the customs officials. By the time that we had finished I was absolutely convinced in my mind that the cargo was one of English files or razors, for it was evidently extraordinarily valuable and not at all bulky, seeing that two "babies" were to carry all the "toys" for a considerable distance. The men, too, were obviously English. I tried the few words of Russian that I knew on them, and their faces remained perfectly blank.

Yes, indeed, I was on the track of M. Aristide Fournier, and of one of the most important hauls of enemy goods which had ever been made in France. Not only that. I had also before me one of the most brutish criminals it had ever been my misfortune to come across. A bully, a fiend of cruelty. In very truth my fertile brain was seething with plans for eventually laying that abominable ruffian by the heels: hanging would be a merciful punishment for such a miscreant. Yes, indeed, five thousand francs—a goodly sum in those days, Sir—was practically assured me. But over and above mere lucre there was the certainty that in a few days' time I should see the light of gratitude shining out of a pair of lustrous blue eyes, and a winning smile chasing away the look of fear and of sorrow from the sweetest face I had seen for many a day.

Despite the turmoil that was raging in my brain, however, I flatter myself that my manner with the rascals remained consistently calm, businesslike, indifferent to all save to the work in hand. The soi-disant Ernest Berty spoke invariably in French, either dictating his orders or seeking information, and I made verbal translation into English of all that he said. The séance lasted close upon an hour, and presently I gathered that the affair was terminated and that I could consider myself dismissed.

I was about to take my leave, having apparently completed my work, when M. Ernest Berty called me back with a curt command.

"One moment, M. Barrot," he said.

"At Monsieur's service," I responded blandly.

"As you see," he continued, "these fellows do not know a word of French. All along the way which they will have to traverse they will meet friendly outposts, who will report to them on the condition of the roads and warn them of any danger that might be ahead. Their ignorance of our language may be a source of infinite peril to them. They need an interpreter to accompany them over the mountains."

He paused for a moment or two, then added abruptly:

"Would you care to go? The matter is important," he went on quietly, "and I am willing to pay you. It means a couple of nights' journey—a halt in the mountains during the day—and there will be ten thousand francs for you if the 'toys' reach St. Claude safely."

I suppose that something in my face betrayed the eagerness which I felt. Here was indeed the finger of Providence pointing to the best means of undoing this abominable criminal. Not that I intended to risk my neck for any ten thousand francs he chose to offer me, but as the trusted guide of his ingenuous "babies" I could convoy them—not to St. Claude, as he blandly believed, but straight into the arms of Leroux and the customs officials.

"Then that is understood," he said in his usual dictatorial manner, taking my consent for granted. "Ten thousand francs. And you will accompany these gentlemen and their 'babies' as far as St. Claude?"

"I am a poor man, Sir," I responded meekly.

"Of course you are," he broke in roughly.

Then from a number of papers which lay upon the table, he selected one which he held out to me.

"Do you know St. Cergues?" he asked.

"Yes," I replied. "It is a short walk from Gex."

"This," he added, pointing to a paper which I had taken from him, "is a plan of the village and of the Pass of Cergues close by. Study it carefully. At some point some way up the pass, which I have marked with a cross, I and my men with the 'babies' will be waiting for you to-morrow evening at eight o'clock. You cannot possibly fail to find the spot, for the plan is very accurate and very minute, and it is less than five hundred metres from the last house at the entrance of the pass. I shall escort the men until then, and hand them over into your charge for the mountain journey. Is that clear?"

"Perfectly."

"Very well, then; you may go. The carriage is outside the door. You know your way."

He dismissed me with a curt nod, and the next two minutes saw me outside this house of mystery and installed inside the ramshackle vehicle on my way back to my lodgings.

I was worn out with fatigue and excitement, and I imagine that I slept most of the way. Certain it is that the journey home was not nearly so long as the outward one had been. The rain was still coming down heavily, but I cared nothing about the weather, nothing about fatigue. My path to fame and fortune had been made easier for me than in my wildest dreams I would have dared to hope. In the morning I would see Leroux and make final arrangements for the capture of those impudent smugglers, and I thought the best way would be for him to meet me and the "babies" and the "toys" at the very outset of our journey, as I did not greatly relish the idea of crossing lonely and dangerous mountain paths in the company of these ruffians.

I reached home without adventure. The vehicle drew up just outside my lodgings, and I was about to alight when my eyes were attracted by something white which lay on the front seat of the carriage, conspicuously placed so that the light from the inside lanthorn fell full upon it. I had been too tired and too dazed, I suppose, to notice the thing before, but now, on closer inspection, I saw that it was a note, and that it was addressed to me: "M. Aristide Barrot, Interpreter," and below my name were the words: "Very urgent."

I took the note feeling a thrill of excitement running through my veins at its touch. I alighted, and the vehicle immediately disappeared into the night. I had only caught one glimpse of the horses, and none at all of the coachman. Then I went straight into my room, and by the light of the table lamp I unfolded and read the mysterious note. It bore no signature, but at the first words I knew that the writer was none other than the lovely young creature who had appeared to me like an angel of innocence in the midst of that den of thieves.

"Monsieur," she had written in a hand which had clearly been trembling with agitation, "you are good, you are kind; I entreat you to be merciful. My dear mother, whom I worship, is sick with terror and misery. She will die if she remains any longer under the sway of that inhuman monster who, alas! is my own brother. And if I lose her I shall die, too, for I should no longer have anyone to stand between me and his cruelties.

"My dear mother has some relations living at St. Claude. She would have gone to them before now, but my brother keeps us both virtual prisoners here, and we have no means of arranging for such a perilous journey for ourselves. Now, by the most extraordinary stroke of good fortune, my brother will be absent all day to-morrow and the following night. My dear mother and I feel that God Himself is showing us the way to our release.

"Will you, can you help us, dear M. Barrot? Mother and I will be at Gex to-morrow at one hour after sundown. We will lie perdu in the little Taverne du Roi de Rome, where, if you come to us, you will find us waiting anxiously. If you can do nothing to help us, we must return broken-hearted to our hated prison; but something in my heart tells me that you can help us. All that we want is a vehicle of some sort and the escort of a brave man like yourself as far as St. Claude, where our relatives will thank you on their knees for your kindness and generosity to two helpless, miserable, unprotected women, and I will kiss your hands in unbounded gratitude and devotion."

It were impossible, Monsieur, to tell you of the varied emotions which filled my heart when I had perused that heart-rending appeal. All my instincts of chivalry were aroused. I was determined to do my duty to these helpless ladies as a man and as a gallant knight. Even before I finally went to bed I had settled in my mind what I meant to do. Fortunately it was quite possible for me to reconcile my duties to my Emperor and those which I owed to myself in the matter of the reward for the apprehension of the smugglers, with my burning desire to be the saviour and protector of the lovely creature whose beauty had inflamed my impressionable heart, and to have my hands kissed by her in gratitude and devotion.

The next morning Leroux and I were deep in our plans, whilst we sipped our coffee outside the Crâne Chauve. He was beside himself with joy and excitement at the prospective haul, which would, of course, redound enormously to his credit, even though the success of the whole undertaking would be due to my acumen, my resourcefulness and my pluck. Fortunately I found him not only ready but eager to render me what assistance he could in the matter of the two ladies who had thrown themselves so entirely on my protection.

"We might get valuable information out of them," he remarked. "In the excess of their gratitude they may betray many more secrets and nefarious doings of the firm of Fournier Frères."

"Which further proves," I remarked, "how deeply you and Monsieur le Ministre of Police are indebted to me over this affair."

He did not argue the point. Indeed, we were both of us far too much excited to waste words in useless bickerings. Our plans for the evening were fairly simple. We both pored over the map which Fournier-Berty had given me, until we felt that we could reach blindfolded the spot which had been marked with a cross. We then arranged that Leroux should betake himself thither with a strong posse of gendarmes during the day, and lie hidden in the vicinity until such time as I myself appeared upon the scene, identified my friends of the night before, parleyed with them for a minute or two, and finally retired, leaving the law in all its majesty, as represented by Leroux, to deal with the rascals.

In the meantime I also mapped out for myself my own share in this night's adventurous work. I had hired a vehicle to take me as far as St. Cergues; here I intended to leave it at the local inn, and then proceed on foot up the mountain pass to the appointed spot. As soon as I had seen the smugglers safely in the hands of Leroux and the gendarmes, I would make my way back to St. Cergues as rapidly as I could, step into my vehicle, drive like the wind back to Gex, and place myself at the disposal of my fair angel and her afflicted mother.

Leroux promised me that at the customs station on the French frontier the officials would look after me and the ladies, and that a pair of fresh horses would be ready to take us straight on to St. Claude, which, if all was well, we could then reach by daybreak.

Having settled all these matters we parted company, he to arrange his own affairs with the Commissary of Police and the customs officials, and I to await with as much patience as I could the hour when I could start for St. Cergues.

4.

The night—just as I anticipated—promised to be very dark. A thin drizzle, which wetted the unfortunate pedestrian to the marrow, had replaced the torrential rain of the previous day.

Twilight was closing in very fast. In the late autumn afternoon I drove to St. Cergues, after which I left the chaise in the village and boldly started to walk up the mountain pass. I had studied the map so carefully that I was quite sure of my way, but though my appointment with the rascals was for eight o'clock, I wished to reach the appointed spot before the last flicker of grey light had disappeared from the sky.

Soon I had left the last house well behind me. Boldly I plunged into the narrow path. The loneliness of the place was indescribable. Every step which I took on the stony track seemed to rouse the echoes of the grim heights which rose precipitously on either side of me, and in my mind I felt aghast at the extraordinary courage of those men who—like Aristide Fournier and his gang— chose to affront such obvious and manifold dangers as these frowning mountain regions held for them for the sake of paltry lucre.

I had walked, according to my reckoning, just upon five hundred metres through the gorge, when on ahead I perceived the flicker of lights which appeared to be moving to and fro. The silence and loneliness no longer seemed to be absolute. A few metres from where I was men were living and breathing, plotting and planning, unconscious of the net which the unerring hand of a skilful fowler had drawn round them and their misdeeds.

The next moment I was challenged by a peremptory "Halt!" Recognition followed. M. Ernest Berty, or Aristide Fournier, whichever he was, acknowledged with a few words my punctuality, whilst through the gloom I took rapid stock of his little party. I saw the vague outline of three men and a couple of mules which appeared to be heavily laden. They were assembled on a flat piece of ground which appeared like a roofless cavern carved out of the mountain side. The walls of rock around them afforded them both cover and refuge. They seemed in no hurry to start. They had the long night before them, so one of them remarked in English.

However, presently M. Fournier-Berty gave the signal for the start to be made, he himself preparing to take leave of his men. Just at that moment my ears caught the welcome sound of the tramping of feet, and before any of the rascals there could realise what was happening, their way was barred by Leroux and his gendarmes, who loudly gave the order, "Hands up, in the name of the Emperor!"

I was only conscious of a confused murmur of voices, of the click of firearms, of words of command passing to and fro, and of several violent oaths uttered in the not unfamiliar voice of M. Aristide Fournier. But already I had spied Leroux. I only exchanged a few words with him, for indeed my share of the evening's work was done as far as he was concerned, and I made haste to retrace my steps through the darkness and the rain along the lonely mountain path toward the goal where chivalry and manly ardour beckoned to me from afar.

I found my vehicle waiting for me at St. Cergues, and by the promise of an additional pourboire, I succeeded in making the driver whip up his horses to some purpose. Less than an hour later we drew up at Gex outside the little inn, pretentiously called Le Roi de Rome. On alighting I was met by the proprietress who, in answer to my inquiry after two ladies who had arrived that afternoon, at once conducted me upstairs.

Already my mind was busy conjuring up visions of the fair lady of yester-eve. The landlady threw open a door and ushered me into a small room which reeked of stale food and damp clothes. I stepped in and found myself face to face with a large and exceedingly ugly old woman who rose with difficulty from the sofa as I entered.

"M. Aristide Barrot," she said as soon as the landlady had closed the door behind me.

"At your service, Madame," I stammered. "But—"

I was indeed almost aghast. Never in my life had I seen anything so grotesque as this woman. To begin with she was more than ordinarily stout and unwieldy—indeed, she appeared like a veritable mountain of flesh; but what was so disturbing to my mind was that she was nothing but a hideous caricature of her lovely daughter, whose dainty features she grotesquely recalled. Her face was seamed and wrinkled, her white hair was plastered down above her yellow forehead. She wore an old-fashioned bonnet tied under her chin, and her huge bulk was draped in a large-patterned cashmere shawl.

"You expected to see my dear daughter beside me, my good M. Barrot," she said after a while speaking with remarkable gentleness and dignity.

"I confess, Madame—" I murmured.

"Ah! the darling has sacrificed herself for my sake. We found to-day that though my son was out of the way, he had set his abominable servants to watch over us. Soon we realized that we could not both get away. It meant one of us staying behind to act the part of unconcern and to throw dust in the eyes of our jailers. My daughter—ah! she is an angel, Monsieur—feared that the disappointment and my son's cruelty, when he returned on the morrow and found that he had been tricked, would seriously endanger my life. She decided that I must go and that she would remain."

"But, Madame—" I protested.

"I know, Monsieur," she rejoined with the same calm dignity which already had commanded my respect, "I know that you think me a selfish old woman; but my Angèle—she is an angel, of a truth!—made all the arrangements, and I could not help but obey her. But have no fears for her safety, Monsieur. My son would not dare lay hands on her as often as he has done on me. Angèle will be brave, and our relations at St. Claude will, directly we arrive, make arrangements to go and fetch her and bring her back to me. My brother is an influential man; he would never have allowed my son to martyrize me and Angèle had he known what we have had to endure."

Of course I could not then tell her that all her fears for herself and the lovely Angèle could now be laid to rest. Her ruffianly son was even now being conveyed by Leroux and his gendarmes to the frontier, where the law would take its course. I was indeed not sorry for him. I was not sorry to think that he would end his evil life upon the guillotine or the gallows. I was only grieved for Angèle who would spend a night and a day, perhaps more, in agonized suspense, knowing nothing of the events which at one great swoop would free her and her beloved mother from the tyranny of a hated brother and send him to expiate his crimes. Not only did I grieve, Sir, for the tender victim of that man's brutality, but I trembled for her safety. I did not know what minions or confederates Fournier-Berty had left in the lonely house yonder, or under what orders they were in case he did not return from his nocturnal expedition.

Indeed for the moment I felt so agitated at thought of that beautiful angel's peril that I looked down with anger and scorn at the fat old woman who ought to have remained beside her daughter to comfort and to shield her.

I was on the point of telling her everything, and dragging her back to her post of duty which she should never have relinquished. Fortunately my sense of what I owed to my own professional dignity prevented my taking such a step. It was clearly not for me to argue. My first duty was to stand by this helpless woman in distress, who had been committed to my charge, and to convey her safely to St. Claude. After which I could see to it that Mademoiselle Angèle was brought along too as quickly as influential relatives could contrive.

In the meanwhile I derived some consolation from the thought that at any rate for the next four and twenty hours the lovely creature would be safe. No news of the arrest of Aristide Fournier could possibly reach the lonely house until I myself could return thither and take her under my protection.

So I said nothing; but with perfect gallantry, just as if fat Mme. Fournier had been a young and beautiful woman, I begged her to give herself the trouble of mounting into the carriage which was waiting for her.

It took time and trouble, Sir, to hoist that mass of solid flesh into the vehicle, and the driver grumbled not a little at the unexpected weight. However, his horses were powerful, wiry, mountain ponies, and we made headway through the darkness and along the smooth, departmental road at moderate speed. I may say that it was a miserably uncomfortable journey for me, sitting, as I was forced to do, on the narrow front seat of the carriage, without support for my head or room for my legs. But Madame's bulk filled the whole of the back seat, and it never seemed to enter her head that I too might like the use of a cushion. However, even the worst moments and the weariest journeys must come to an end, and we reached the frontier in the small hours of the morning. Here we found the customs officials ready to render us any service we might require. Leroux had not failed to order the fresh relay of horses, and whilst these were being put to, the polite officers of the station gave Madame and myself some excellent coffee. Beyond the formal: "Madame has nothing to declare for His Majesty's customs?" and my companion's equally formal: "Nothing, Monsieur, except my personal belongings," they did not ply us with questions, and after half an hour's halt we again proceeded on our way.

We reached St. Claude at daybreak, and following Madame's directions, the driver pulled up in front of a large house in the Avenue du Jura. Again there was the same difficulty in hoisting the unwieldy lady out of the vehicle, but this time, in response to my vigorous pull at the outside bell, the concierge and another man came out of the house, and very respectfully they approached Madame and conveyed her into the house.

While they did so she apparently gave them some directions about myself, for anon the concierge returned, and with extreme politeness told me that Madame Fournier greatly hoped that I would stay in St. Claude a day or two as she had the desire to see me again very soon. She also honoured me with an invitation to dine with her that same evening at seven of the clock. This was the first time, I noticed, that the name Fournier was actually used in connexion with any of the people with whom I had become so dramatically involved. Not that I had ever doubted the identity of the ruffianly Ernest Berty; still it was very satisfactory to have my surmises confirmed. I concluded that the fine house in the Avenue du Jura belonged to Mme. Fournier's brother, and I vaguely wondered who he was. The invitation to dinner had certainly been given in her name, and the servants had received her with a show of respect which suggested that she was more than a guest in her brother's house.

Be that as it may, I betook myself for the nonce to the Hôtel des Moines in the centre of the town and killed time for the rest of the day as best I could. For one thing I needed rest after the emotions and the fatigue of the past forty-eight hours. Remember, Sir, I had not slept for two nights and had spent the last eight hours on the narrow front seat of a jolting chaise. So I had a good rest in the afternoon, and at seven o'clock I presented myself once more at the house in the Avenue du Jura.

My intention was to retire early to bed after spending an agreeable evening with the family, who would no doubt overwhelm me with their gratitude, and at daybreak I would drive back to Gex after I had heard all the latest news from Leroux.

I confess that it was with a pardonable feeling of agitation that I tugged at the wrought-iron bell-pull on the perron of the magnificent mansion in the Avenue du Jura. To begin with I felt somewhat rueful at having to appear before ladies at this hour in my travelling clothes, and then, you will admit, Sir, that it was a somewhat awkward predicament for a man of highly sensitive temperament to meet on terms of equality a refined if stout lady whose son he had just helped to send to the gallows. Fortunately there was no likelihood of Mme. Fournier being as yet aware of this unpleasant fact: even if she did know at this hour that her son's illicit adventure had come to grief, she could not possibly in her mind connect me with his ill-fortune. So I allowed the sumptuous valet to take my hat and coat and I followed him with as calm a demeanour as I could assume up the richly carpeted stairs. Obviously the relatives of Mme. Fournier were more than well to do. Everything in the house showed evidences of luxury, not to say wealth. I was ushered into an elegant salon wherein every corner showed traces of dainty feminine hands. There were embroidered silk cushions upon the sofa, lace covers upon the tables, whilst a work basket, filled with a riot of many coloured silks, stood invitingly open. And through the apartment, Sir, a scent of violets lingered and caressed my nostrils, reminding me of a beauteous creature in distress whom it had been my good fortune to succour.

I had waited less than five minutes when I heard a swift, elastic step approaching through the next room, and a second or so later, before I had time to take up an appropriate posture, the door was thrown open and the exquisite vision of my waking dreams—the beautiful Angèle— stood smiling before me.

"Mademoiselle," I stammered somewhat clumsily, for of a truth I was hardly able to recover my breath, and surprise had well nigh robbed me of speech, "how comes it that you are here?"

She only smiled in reply, the most adorable smile I had ever seen on any human face, so full of joy, of mischief—aye, of triumph, was it. I asked after Madame. Again she smiled, and said Madame was in her room, resting from the fatigues of her journey. I had scarce recovered from my initial surprise when another—more complete still—confronted me. This was the appearance of Monsieur Aristide Fournier, whom I had fondly imagined already expiating his crimes in a frontier prison, but who now entered, also smiling, also extremely pleasant, who greeted me as if we were lifelong friends, and who then—I scarce could believe my eyes—placed his arm affectionately round his sister's waist, while she turned her sweet face up to his and gave him a fond—nay, a loving look. A loving look to him who was a brute and a bully and a miscreant amenable to the gallows! True his appearance was completely changed: his eyes were bright and kindly, his mouth continued to smile, his manner was urbane in the extreme when he finally introduced himself to me as: "Aristide Fournier, my dear Monsieur Ratichon, at your service."

He knew my name, he knew who I was! whilst I . . . I had to pass my hand once or twice over my forehead and to close and reopen my eyes several times, for, of a truth, it all seemed like a dream. I tried to stammer out a question or two, but I could only gasp, and the lovely Angèle appeared highly amused at my distress.

"Let us dine," she said gaily, "after which you may ask as many questions as you like."

In very truth I was in no mood for dinner. Puzzlement and anxiety appeared to grip me by the throat and to choke me. It was all very well for the beautiful creature to laugh and to make merry. She had cruelly deceived me, played upon the chords of my sensitive heart for purposes which no doubt would presently be made clear, but in the meanwhile since the smuggling of the English files had been successful—as it apparently was—what had become of Leroux and his gendarmes?

What tragedy had been enacted in the narrow gorge of St. Cergues, and what, oh! what had become of my hopes of that five thousand francs for the apprehension of the smugglers, promised me by Leroux? Can you wonder that for the moment the very thought of dinner was abhorrent to me? But only for the moment. The next a sumptuous valet had thrown open the folding-doors, and down the vista of the stately apartment I perceived a table richly laden with china and glass and silver, whilst a distinctly savoury odour was wafted to my nostrils.

"We will not answer a single question," the fair Angèle reiterated with adorable determination, "until after we have dined."

What, Sir, would you have done in my place? I believe that never until this hour had Hector Ratichon reached to such a sublimity of manner. I bowed with perfect dignity in token of obedience to the fair creature, Sir; then without a word I offered her my arm. She placed her hand upon it, and I conducted her to the dining-room, whilst Aristide Fournier, who at this hour should have been on a fair way to being hanged, followed in our wake.

Ah! it seemed indeed a lovely dream: one that lasted through an excellent and copious dinner, and which turned to delightful reality when, over a final glass of succulent Madeira, Monsieur Aristide Fournier slowly counted out one hundred notes, worth one hundred francs each, and presented these to me with a gracious nod.

"Your fee, Monsieur," he said, "and allow me to say that never have I paid out so large a sum with such a willing hand."

"But I have done nothing," I murmured from out the depths of my bewilderment.

Mademoiselle Angèle and Monsieur Fournier looked at one another, and, no doubt, I presented a very comical spectacle; for both of them burst into an uncontrollable fit of laughter.

"Indeed, Monsieur," quoth Monsieur Fournier as soon as he could speak coherently, "you have done everything that you set out to do and done it with perfect chivalry. You conveyed 'the toys' safely over the frontier as far as St. Claude."

"But how?" I stammered, "how?"

Again Mademoiselle Angèle laughed, and through the ripples of her laughter came her merry words:

"Maman was very fat, was she not, my good Monsieur Ratichon? Did you not think she was extraordinarily like me?"

I caught the glance in her eyes, and they were literally glowing with mischief. Then all of a sudden I understood. She had impersonated a fat mother, covered her lovely face with lines, worn a disfiguring wig and an antiquated bonnet, and round her slender figure she had tucked away thousands of packages of English files. I could only gasp. Astonishment, not to say admiration, at her pluck literally took my breath away.

"But, Monsieur Berty?" I murmured, my mind in a turmoil, my thoughts running riot through my brain. "The Englishmen, the mules, the packs?"

"Monsieur Berty, as you see, stands before you now in the person of Monsieur Fournier," she replied. "The Englishmen were three faithful servants who threw dust not only in your eyes, my dear M. Ratichon, but in those of the customs officials, while the packs contained harmless personal luggage which was taken by your friend and his gendarmes to the customs station at Mijoux, and there, after much swearing, equally solemnly released with many apologies to M. Fournier, who was allowed to proceed unmolested on his way, and who arrived here safely this afternoon, whilst Maman divested herself of her fat and once more became the slender Mme. Aristide Fournier, at your service."

She bobbed me a dainty curtsy, and I could only try and hide the pain which this last cruel stab had inflicted on my heart. So she was not "Mademoiselle" after all, and henceforth it would even be wrong to indulge in dreams of her.

But the ten thousand francs crackled pleasantly in my breast pocket, and when I finally took leave of Monsieur Aristide Fournier and his charming wife, I was an exceedingly happy man.

But Leroux never forgave me. Of what he suspected me I do not know, or if he suspected me at all. He certainly must have known about fat Maman from the customs officials who had given us coffee at Mijoux.

But he never mentioned the subject to me at all, nor has he spoken to me since that memorable night. To one of his colleagues he once said that no words in his vocabulary could possibly be adequate to express his feelings.

CHAPTER VI

HONOUR AMONG ——

1.

Ah, my dear Sir, it is easy enough to despise our profession, but believe me that all the finer qualities—those of loyalty and of truth—are essential, not only to us, but to our subordinates, if we are to succeed in making even a small competence out of it.

Now let me give you an instance. Here was I, Hector Ratichon, settled in Paris in that eventful year 1816 which saw the new order of things finally swept aside and the old order resume its triumphant sway, which saw us all, including our God-given King Louis XVIII, as poor as the proverbial church mice and as eager for a bit of comfort and luxury as a hungry dog is for a bone; the year which saw the army disbanded and hordes of unemployed and unemployable men wandering disconsolate and half starved through the country seeking in vain for some means of livelihood, while the Allied troops, well fed and well clothed, stalked about as if the sacred soil of France was so much dirt under their feet; the year, my dear Sir, during which more intrigues were hatched and more plots concocted than in any previous century in the whole history of France. We were all trying to make money, since there was so precious little of it about. Those of us who had brains succeeded, and then not always.

Now, I had brains—I do not boast of them; they are a gift from Heaven—but I had them, and good looks, too, and a general air of strength, coupled with refinement, which was bound to appeal to anyone needing help and advice, and willing to pay for both, and yet—but you shall judge.

You know my office in the Rue Daunou, you have been in it—plainly furnished; but, as I said, these were not days of luxury. There was an antechamber, too, where that traitor, blackmailer and thief, Theodore, my confidential clerk in those days, lodged at my expense and kept importunate clients at bay for what was undoubtedly a liberal salary—ten per cent, on all the profits of the business—and yet he was always complaining, the ungrateful, avaricious brute!

Well, Sir, on that day in September—it was the tenth, I remember—1816, I must confess that I was feeling exceedingly dejected. Not one client for the last three weeks, half a franc in my pocket, and nothing but a small quarter of Strasburg patty in the larder. Theodore had eaten most of it, and I had just sent him out to buy two sous' worth of stale bread wherewith to finish the remainder. But after that? You will admit, Sir, that a less buoyant spirit would not have remained so long undaunted.

I was just cursing that lout Theodore inwardly, for he had been gone half an hour, and I strongly suspected him of having spent my two sous on a glass of absinthe, when there was a ring at the door, and I, Hector Ratichon, the confidant of kings and intimate counsellor of half the aristocracy in the kingdom, was forced to go and open the door just like a common lackey.

But here the sight which greeted my eyes fully compensated me for the temporary humiliation, for on the threshold stood a gentleman who had wealth written plainly upon his fine clothes, upon the dainty linen at his throat and wrists, upon the quality of his rich satin necktie and the perfect set of his fine cloth pantaloons, which were of an exquisite shade of dove-grey. When, then, the apparition spoke, inquiring with just a sufficiency of aristocratic hauteur whether M. Hector Ratichon were in, you cannot be surprised, my dear Sir, that my dejection fell from me like a cast-off mantle and that all my usual urbanity of manner returned to me as I informed the elegant gentleman that M. Ratichon was even now standing before him, and begged him to take the trouble to pass through into my office.

This he did, and I placed a chair in position for him. He sat down, having previously dusted the chair with a graceful sweep of his lace-edged handkerchief. Then he raised a gold-rimmed eyeglass to his right eye with a superlatively elegant gesture, and surveyed me critically for a moment or two ere he said:

"I am told, my good M. Ratichon, that you are a trustworthy fellow, and one who is willing to undertake a delicate piece of business for a moderate honorarium."

Except for the fact that I did not like the word "moderate," I was enchanted with him.

"Rumour for once has not lied, Monsieur," I replied in my most attractive manner.

"Well," he rejoined—I won't say curtly, but with businesslike brevity, "for all purposes connected with the affair which I desire to treat with you my name, as far as you are concerned, shall be Jean Duval. Understand?"

"Perfectly, Monsieur le Marquis," I replied with a bland smile.

It was a wild guess, but I don't think that I underestimated my new client's rank, for he did not wince.

"You know Mlle. Mars?" he queried.

"The actress?" I replied. "Perfectly."

"She is playing in *Le Rêve* at the Theatre Royal just now."

"She is."

"In the first and third acts of the play she wears a gold bracelet set with large green stones."

"I noticed it the other night. I had a seat in the parterre, I may say."

"I want that bracelet," broke in the soi-disant Jean Duval unceremoniously. "The stones are false, the gold strass. I admire Mlle. Mars immensely. I dislike seeing her wearing false jewellery. I wish to have the bracelet copied in real stones, and to present it to her as a surprise on the occasion of the twenty-fifth performance of *Le Rêve*. It will cost me a king's ransom, and her, for the time being, an infinite amount of anxiety. She sets great store by the valueless trinket solely because of the merit of its design, and I want its disappearance to have every semblance of a theft. All the greater will be the lovely creature's pleasure when, at my hands, she will receive an infinitely precious jewel the exact counterpart in all save its intrinsic value of the trifle which she had thought lost."

It all sounded deliciously romantic. A flavour of the past century—before the endless war and abysmal poverty had killed all chivalry in us—clung to this proposed transaction. There was nothing of the roturier, nothing of a Jean Duval, in this polished man of the world who had thought out this subtle scheme for ingratiating himself in the eyes of his lady fair.

I murmured an appropriate phrase, placing my services entirely at M. le Marquis's disposal, and once more he broke in on my polished diction with that brusquerie which betrayed the man accustomed to be silently obeyed.

"Mlle. Mars wears the bracelet," he said, "during the third act of *Le Rêve*. At the end of the act she enters her dressing-room, and her maid helps her to change her dress. During this entr'acte Mademoiselle with her own hands puts by all the jewellery which she has to wear during the more gorgeous scenes of the play. In the last act—the finale of the tragedy—she appears in a plain stuff gown, whilst all her jewellery reposes in the small iron safe in her dressing-room. It is while Mademoiselle is on the stage during the last act that I want you to enter her dressing-room and to extract the bracelet out of the safe for me."

"I, M. le Marquis?" I stammered. "I, to steal a—"

"Firstly, M.—er—er—Ratichon, or whatever your confounded name may be," interposed my client with inimitable hauteur, "understand that my name is Jean Duval, and if you forget this again I shall be under the necessity of laying my cane across your shoulders and incidentally to take my business elsewhere. Secondly, let me tell you that your affectations of outraged probity are lost on me, seeing that I know all about the stolen treaty which—"

"Enough, M. Jean Duval," I said with a dignity equal, if not greater, than his own; "do not, I pray you, misunderstand me. I am ready to do you service. But if you will deign to explain how I am to break open an iron safe inside a crowded building and extract therefrom a trinket, without being caught in the act and locked up for house-breaking and theft, I shall be eternally your debtor."

"The extracting of the trinket is your affair," he rejoined dryly. "I will give you five hundred francs if you bring the bracelet to me within fourteen days."

"But—" I stammered again.

"Your task will not be such a difficult one after all. I will give you the duplicate key of the safe."

He dived into the breast pocket of his coat, and drew from it a somewhat large and clumsy key, which he placed upon my desk.

"I managed to get that easily enough," he said nonchalantly, "a couple of nights ago, when I had the honour of visiting Mademoiselle in her dressing-room. A piece of wax in my hand, Mademoiselle's momentary absorption in her reflection while her maid was doing her hair, and the impression of the original key was in my possession. But between taking a model of the key and the actual theft of the bracelet out of the safe there is a wide gulf which a gentleman cannot bridge over. Therefore, I choose to employ you, M.—er—er—Ratichon, to complete the transaction for me."

"For five hundred francs?" I queried blandly.

"It is a fair sum," he argued.

"Make it a thousand," I rejoined firmly, "and you shall have the bracelet within fourteen days."

He paused a moment in order to reflect; his steel-grey eyes, cool and disdainful, were fixed searchingly on my face. I pride myself on the way that I bear that kind of scrutiny, so even now I looked bland and withal purposeful and capable.

"Very well," he said, after a few moments, and he rose from his chair as he spoke; "it shall be a thousand francs, M.—er—er—Ratichon, and I will hand over the money to you in exchange for the bracelet—but it must be done within fourteen days, remember."

I tried to induce him to give me a small sum on account. I was about to take terrible risks, remember; housebreaking, larceny, theft—call it what you will, it meant the *police correctionelle* and a couple of years in New Orleans for sure. He finally gave me fifty francs, and once more threatened to take his business elsewhere, so I had to accept and to look as urbane and dignified as I could.

He was out of the office and about to descend the stairs when a thought struck me.

"Where and how can I communicate with M. Jean Duval," I asked, "when my work is done?"

"I will call here," he replied, "at ten o'clock of every morning that follows a performance of *Le Rêve*. We can complete our transaction then across your office desk."

The next moment he was gone. Theodore passed him on the stairs and asked me, with one of his impertinent leers, whether we had a new client and what we might expect from him. I shrugged my shoulders. "A new client!" I said disdainfully. "Bah! Vague promises of a couple of louis for finding out if Madame his wife sees more of a certain captain of the guards than Monsieur the husband cares about."

Theodore sniffed. He always sniffs when financial matters are on the tapis.

"Anything on account?" he queried.

"A paltry ten francs," I replied, "and I may as well give you your share of it now."

I tossed a franc to him across the desk. By the terms of my contract with him, you understand, he was entitled to ten per cent, of every profit accruing from the business in lieu of wages, but in this instance do you not think that I was justified in looking on one franc now, and perhaps twenty when the transaction was completed, as a more than just honorarium for his share in it? Was I not taking all the risks in this delicate business? Would it be fair for me to give him a hundred francs for sitting quietly in the office or sipping absinthe at a neighbouring bar whilst I risked New Orleans—not to speak of the gallows?

He gave me a strange look as he picked up the silver franc, spat on it for luck, bit it with his great yellow teeth to ascertain if it were counterfeit or genuine, and finally slipped it into his pocket, and shuffled out of the office whistling through his teeth.

An abominably low, deceitful creature, that Theodore, you will see anon. But I won't anticipate.

2.

The next performance of *Le Rêve* was announced for the following evening, and I started on my campaign. As you may imagine, it did not prove an easy matter. To obtain access through the stage-door to the back of the theatre was one thing—a franc to the doorkeeper had done the trick—to mingle with the scene-shifters, to talk with the supers, to take off my hat with every form of deep respect to the principals had been equally simple.

I had even succeeded in placing a bouquet on the dressing-table of the great tragedienne on my second visit to the theatre. Her dressing-room door had been left ajar during that memorable fourth act which was to see the consummation of my labours. I had the bouquet in my hand, having brought it expressly for that purpose. I pushed open the door, and found myself face to face with a young though somewhat forbidding damsel, who peremptorily demanded what my business might be.

In order to minimise the risk of subsequent trouble, I had assumed the disguise of a middle-aged Angliche—red side-whiskers, florid complexion, a ginger-coloured wig plastered rigidly over the ears towards the temples, high stock collar, nankeen pantaloons, a patch over one eye and an eyeglass fixed in the other. My own sainted mother would never have known me.

With becoming diffidence I explained in broken French that my deep though respectful admiration of Mlle. Mars had prompted me to lay a floral tribute at her feet. I desired nothing more.

The damsel eyed me coldly, though at the moment I was looking quite my best, diffident yet courteous, a perfect gentleman of the old regime. Then she took the bouquet from me and put it down on the dressing-table.

I fancied that she smiled, not unkindly, and I ventured to pass the time of day. She replied not altogether disapprovingly. She sat down by the dressing-table and took up some needlework which she had obviously thrown aside on my arrival. Close by, on the floor, was a solid iron chest with huge ornamental hinges and a large escutcheon over the lock. It stood about a foot high and perhaps a couple of feet long.

There was nothing else in the room that suggested a receptacle for jewellery; this, therefore, was obviously the safe which contained the bracelet. At the self-same second my eyes alighted on a large and clumsy-looking key which lay upon the dressing-table, and my hand at once wandered instinctively to the pocket of my coat and closed convulsively on the duplicate one which the soi-disant Jean Duval had given me.

I talked eloquently for a while. The damsel answered in monosyllables, but she sat unmoved at needlework, and after ten minutes or so I was forced to beat a retreat.

I returned to the charge at the next performance of *Le Rêve*, this time with a box of bonbons for the maid instead of the bouquet for the mistress. The damsel was quite amenable to a little conversation, quite willing that I should dally in her company. She munched the bonbons and coquetted a little with me. But she went on stolidly with her needlework, and I could see that nothing would move her out of that room, where she had obviously been left in charge.

Then I bethought me of Theodore. I realised that I could not carry this affair through successfully without his help. So I gave him a further five francs—as I said to him it was out of my own savings—and I assured him that a certain M. Jean Duval had promised me a couple of hundred francs when the business which he had entrusted to me was satisfactorily concluded. It was for this business—so I explained—that I required his help, and he seemed quite satisfied.

His task was, of course, a very easy one. What a contrast to the risk I was about to run! Twenty-five francs, my dear Sir, just for knocking at the door of Mlle. Mars' dressing-room during the fourth act, whilst I was engaged in conversation with the attractive guardian of the iron safe, and to say in well-assumed, breathless tones:

"Mademoiselle Mars has been taken suddenly unwell on the stage. Will her maid go to her at once?"

It was some little distance from the dressing-room to the wings—down a flight of ill-lighted stone stairs which demanded cautious ascent and descent. Theodore had orders to obstruct the maid during her progress as much as he could without rousing her suspicions.

I reckoned that she would be fully three minutes going, questioning, finding out that the whole thing was a hoax, and running back to the dressing-room—three minutes in which to open the chest, extract the bracelet and, incidentally, anything else of value there might be close to my hand. Well, I had thought of that eventuality, too; one must think of everything, you know—that is where genius comes in. Then, if possible, relock the safe, so that the maid, on her return, would find everything apparently in order and would not, perhaps, raise the alarm until I was safely out of the theatre.

It could be done—oh, yes, it could be done—with a minute to spare! And to-morrow at ten o'clock M. Jean Duval would appear, and I would not part with the bracelet until a thousand francs had passed from his pocket into mine. I must get Theodore out of the house, by the way, before the arrival of M. Duval.

A thousand francs! I had not seen a thousand francs all at once for years. What a dinner I would have tomorrow! There was a certain little restaurant in the Rue des Pipots where they concocted a cassolette of goose liver and pork chops with haricot beans which . . . ! I only tell you that.

How I got through the rest of that day I cannot tell you. The evening found me—quite an habitué now—behind the stage of the Theatre Royal, nodding to one or two acquaintants, most of the people looking on me with grave respect and talking of me as the eccentric milor. I was supposed to be pining for an introduction to the great tragedienne, who, very exclusive as usual, had so far given me the cold shoulder.

Ten minutes after the rise of the curtain on the fourth act I was in the dressing-room, presenting the maid with a gold locket which I had bought from a cheapjack's barrow for five and twenty francs—almost the last of the fifty which I had received from M. Duval on account. The damsel was eyeing the locket somewhat disdainfully and giving me grudging thanks for it when there came a hurried knock at the door. The next moment Theodore poked his ugly face into the room. He, too, had taken the precaution of assuming an excellent disguise—peaked cap set aslant over one eye, grimy face, the blouse of a scene-shifter.

"Mlle. Mars," he gasped breathlessly; "she has been taken ill—on the stage—very suddenly. She is in the wings—asking for her maid. They think she will faint."

The damsel rose, visibly frightened.

"I'll come at once," she said, and without the slightest flurry she picked up the key of the safe and slipped it into her pocket. I fancied that she gave me a look as she did this. Oh, she was a pearl among Abigails! Then she pointed unceremoniously to the door.

"Milor!" was all she said, but of course I understood. I had no idea that English milors could be thus treated by pert maidens. But what cared I for social amenities just then? My hand had closed over the duplicate key of the safe, and I walked out of the room in the wake of the damsel. Theodore had disappeared.

Once in the passage, the girl started to run. A second or two later I heard the patter of her high-heeled shoes down the stone stairs. I had not a moment to lose.

To slip back into the dressing-room was but an instant's work. The next I was kneeling in front of the chest. The key fitted the lock accurately; one turn, and the lid flew open.

The chest was filled with a miscellaneous collection of theatrical properties all lying loose—showy necklaces, chains, pendants, all of them obviously false; but lying beneath them, and partially hidden by the meretricious ornaments, were one or two boxes covered with velvet such as jewellers use. My keen eyes noted these at once. I was indeed in luck! For the moment, however, my hand fastened on a leather case which reposed on the top in one corner, and which very obviously, from its shape, contained a bracelet. My hands did not tremble, though I was quivering with excitement. I opened the case. There, indeed, was the bracelet—the large green stones, the magnificent gold setting, the whole jewel dazzlingly beautiful. If it were real—the thought flashed through my mind—it would be indeed priceless. I closed the case and put it on the dressing-table beside me. I had at least another minute to spare—sixty seconds wherein to dive for those velvet-covered boxes which— My hand was on one of them when a slight noise caused me suddenly to turn and to look behind me. It all happened as quickly as a flash of lightning. I just saw a man disappearing through the door. One glance at the dressing-table showed me the whole extent of my misfortune. The case containing the bracelet had gone, and at that precise moment I heard a commotion from the direction of the stairs and a woman screaming at the top of her voice: "Thief! Stop thief!"

Then, Sir, I brought upon the perilous situation that presence of mind for which the name of Hector Ratichon will for ever remain famous. Without a single flurried movement, I slipped one of the velvet-covered cases which I still had in my hand into the breast pocket of my coat, I closed down the lid of the iron chest and locked it with the duplicate key, and I went out of the room, closing the door behind me.

The passage was dark. The damsel was running up the stairs with a couple of stage hands behind her. She was explaining to them volubly, and to the accompaniment of sundry half-hysterical little cries, the infamous hoax to which she had fallen a victim. You might think, Sir, that here was I caught like a rat in a trap, and with that velvet-covered case in my breast pocket by way of damning evidence against me!

Not at all, Sir! Not at all! Not so is Hector Ratichon, the keenest secret agent France has ever known, the confidant of kings, brought to earth by an untoward move of fate. Even before the damsel and the stage hands had reached the top of the stairs and turned into the corridor, which was on my left, I had slipped round noiselessly to my right and found shelter in a narrow doorway, where I was screened by the surrounding darkness and by a projection of the frame. While the three of them made straight for Mademoiselle's dressing-room, and spent some considerable time there in uttering varied ejaculations when they found the place and the chest to all appearances untouched, I slipped out of my hiding-place, sped rapidly along the corridor, and was soon half-way down the stairs.

Here my habitual composure in the face of danger stood me in good stead. It enabled me to walk composedly and not too hurriedly through the crowd behind the scenes—supers, scene-shifters, principals, none of whom seemed to be aware as yet of the hoax practised on Mademoiselle Mars' maid; and I reckon that I was out of the stage door exactly five minutes after Theodore had called the damsel away.

But I was minus the bracelet, and in my mind there was the firm conviction that that traitor Theodore had played me one of his abominable tricks. As I said, the whole thing had occurred as quickly as a flash of lightning, but even so my keen, experienced eyes had retained the impression of a peaked cap and the corner of a blue blouse as they disappeared through the dressing-room door.

3.

Tact, wariness and strength were all required, you must admit, in order to deal with the present delicate situation. I was speeding along the Rue de Richelieu on my way to my office. My intention was to spend the night there, where I had a chair-bedstead on which I had oft before slept soundly after a day's hard work, and anyhow it was too late to go to my lodgings at Passy at this hour.

Moreover, Theodore slept in the antechamber of the office, and I was more firmly convinced than ever that it was he who had stolen the bracelet. "Blackleg! Thief! Traitor!" I mused. "But thou hast not done with Hector Ratichon yet."

In the meanwhile I bethought me of the velvet-covered box in my breast pocket, and of the ginger-coloured hair and whiskers that I was still wearing, and which might prove an unpleasant "piece de conviction" in case the police were after the stolen bracelet.

With a view to examining the one and getting rid of the other, I turned into the Square Louvois, which, as usual, was very dark and wholly deserted. Here I took off my wig and whiskers and threw them over the railings into the garden. Then I drew the velvet-covered box from my pocket, opened it, and groped for its contents. Imagine my feelings, my dear Sir, when I realised that the case was empty! Fate was indeed against me that night. I had been fooled and cheated by a traitor, and had risked New Orleans and worse for an empty box.

For a moment I must confess that I lost that imperturbable sang-froid which is the admiration of all my friends, and with a genuine oath I flung the case over the railings in the wake of the milor's hair and whiskers. Then I hurried home.

Theodore had not returned. He did not come in until the small hours of the morning, and then he was in a state that I can only describe, with your permission, as hoggish. He could hardly speak. I had him at my mercy. Neither tact nor wariness was required for the moment. I stripped him to his skin; he only laughed like an imbecile. His eyes had a horrid squint in them; he was hideous. I found five francs in one of his pockets, but neither in his clothes nor on his person did I find the bracelet.

"What have you done with it?" I cried, for by this time I was maddened with rage.

"I don't know what you are talking about!" he stammered thickly, as he tottered towards his bed. "Give me back my five francs, you thief!" the brutish creature finally blurted out ere he fell into a hog-like sleep.

4.

Desperate evils need desperate remedies. I spent the rest of the night thinking hard. By the time that dawn was breaking my mind was made up. Theodore's stertorous breathing assured me that he was still insentient. I was muscular in those days, and he a meagre, attenuated, drink-sodden creature. I lifted him out of his bed in the antechamber and carried him into mine in the office. I found a coil of rope, and strapped him tightly in the chair-bedstead so that he could not move. I tied a scarf round his mouth so that he could not scream. Then, at six o'clock, when the humbler eating-houses begin to take down their shutters, I went out.

I had Theodore's five francs in my pocket, and I was desperately hungry. I spent ten sous on a cup of coffee and a plate of fried onions and haricot beans, and three francs on a savoury pie, highly flavoured with garlic, and a quarter-bottle of excellent cognac. I drank the coffee and ate the onions and the beans, and I took the pie and cognac home.

I placed a table close to the chair-bedstead and on it I disposed the pie and the cognac in such a manner that the moment Theodore woke his eyes were bound to alight on them. Then I waited. I absolutely ached to have a taste of that pie myself, it smelt so good, but I waited.

Theodore woke at nine o'clock. He struggled like a fool, but he still appeared half dazed. No doubt he thought that he was dreaming. Then I sat down on the edge of the bed and cut myself off a large piece of the pie. I ate it with marked relish in front of Theodore, whose eyes nearly started out of their sockets. Then I brewed myself a cup of coffee. The mingled odour of coffee and garlic filled the room. It was delicious. I thought that Theodore would have a fit. The veins stood out on his forehead and a kind of gurgle came from behind the scarf round his mouth. Then I told him he could partake of the pie and coffee if he told me what he had done with the bracelet. He shook his head furiously, and I left the pie, the cognac and the coffee on the table before him and went into the antechamber, closing the office door behind me, and leaving him to meditate on his treachery.

What I wanted to avoid above everything was the traitor meeting M. Jean Duval. He had the bracelet—of that I was as convinced as that I was alive. But what could he do with a piece of false jewellery? He could not dispose of it, save to a vendor of theatrical properties, who no doubt was well acquainted with the trinket and would not give more than a couple of francs for what was obviously stolen property. After all, I had promised Theodore twenty francs; he would not be such a fool as to sell that birthright for a mess of pottage and the sole pleasure of doing me a bad turn.

There was no doubt in my mind that he had put the thing away somewhere in what he considered a safe place pending a reward being offered by Mlle. Mars for the recovery of the bracelet. The more I thought of this the more convinced I was that that was, indeed, his proposed plan of action—oh, how I loathed the blackleg!—and mine henceforth would be to dog his every footstep and never let him out of my sight until I forced him to disgorge his ill-gotten booty.

At ten o'clock M. Jean Duval arrived, as was his wont, supercilious and brusque as usual. I was just explaining to him that I hoped to have excellent news for him after the next performance of Le Rêve when there was a peremptory ring at the bell. I went to open the door, and there stood a police inspector in uniform with a sheaf of papers in his hand.

Now, I am not over-fond of our Paris police; they poke their noses in where they are least wanted. Their incompetence favours the machinations of rogues and frustrates the innocent ambitions of the just. However, in this instance the inspector looked amiable enough, though his manner, I must say, was, as usual, unpleasantly curt.

"Here, Ratichon," he said, "there has been an impudent theft of a valuable bracelet out of Mademoiselle Mars' dressing-room at the Theatre Royal last night. You and your mate frequent all sorts of places of ill-fame; you may hear something of the affair."

I chose to ignore the insult, and the inspector detached a paper from the sheaf which he held and threw it across the table to me.

"There is a reward of two thousand five hundred francs," he said, "for the recovery of the bracelet. You will find on that paper an accurate description of the jewel. It contains the celebrated Maroni emerald, presented to the ex-Emperor by the Sultan, and given by him to Mlle. Mars."

Whereupon he turned unceremoniously on his heel and went, leaving me face to face with the man who had so shamefully tried to swindle me. I turned, and resting my elbow on the table and my chin in my hand, I looked mutely on the soi-disant Jean Duval and equally mutely pointed with an accusing finger to the description of the famous bracelet which he had declared to me was merely strass and base metal.

But he had the impudence to turn on me before I could utter a syllable.

"Where is the bracelet?" he demanded. "You consummate liar, you! Where is it? You stole it last night! What have you done with it?"

"I extracted, at your request," I replied with as much dignity as I could command, "a piece of theatrical jewellery, which you stated to me to be worthless, out of an iron chest, the key of which you placed in my hands. I . . ."

"Enough of this rubbish!" he broke in roughly. "You have the bracelet. Give it me now, or . . ."

He broke off and looked somewhat alarmed in the direction of the office door, from the other side of which there had just come a loud crash, followed by loud, if unintelligible, vituperation. What had happened I could not guess; all that I could do was to carry off the situation as boldly as I dared.

"You shall have the bracelet, Sir," I said in my most suave manner. "You shall have it, but not unless you will pay me three thousand francs for it. I can get two thousand five hundred by taking it straight to Mlle. Mars."

"And be taken up by the police for stealing it," he retorted. "How will you explain its being in your possession?"

I did not blanch.

"That is my affair," I replied. "Will you give me three thousand francs for it? It is worth sixty thousand francs to a clever thief like you."

"You hound!" he cried, livid with rage, and raised his cane as if he would strike me.

"Aye, it was cleverly done, M. Jean Duval, whoever you may be. I know that the gentleman-thief is a modern product of the old regime, but I did not know that the fraternity could show such a fine specimen as yourself. Pay Hector Ratichon a thousand francs for stealing a bracelet for you worth sixty! Indeed, M. Jean Duval, you deserved to succeed!"

Again he shook his cane at me.

"If you touch me," I declared boldly, "I shall take the bracelet at once to Mlle. Mars."

He bit his lip and made a great effort to pull himself together.

"I haven't three thousand francs by me," he said.

"Go, fetch the money," I retorted, "and I'll fetch the bracelet."

He demurred for a while, but I was firm, and after he had threatened to thrash me, to knock me down, and to denounce me to the police, he gave in and went to fetch the money.

5.

When I remembered Theodore—Theodore, whom only a thin partition wall had separated from the full knowledge of the value of his ill-gotten treasure!—I could have torn my hair out by the roots with the magnitude of my rage. He, the traitor, the blackleg, was about to triumph, where I, Hector Ratichon, had failed! He had but to take the bracelet to Mlle. Mars himself and obtain the munificent reward whilst I, after I had taken so many risks and used all the brains and tact wherewith Nature had endowed me, would be left with the meagre remnants of the fifty francs which M. Jean Duval had so grudgingly thrown to me. Twenty-five francs for a gold locket, ten francs for a bouquet, another ten for bonbons, and five for gratuities to the stage-doorkeeper! Make the calculation, my good Sir, and see what I had left. If it had not been for the five francs which I had found in Theodore's pocket last night, I would at this moment not only have been breakfastless, but also absolutely penniless.

As it was, my final hope—and that a meagre one—was to arouse one spark of honesty in the breast of the arch-traitor, and either by cajolery or threats, to induce him to share his ill-gotten spoils with me.

I had left him snoring and strapped to the chair-bedstead, and when I opened the office door I was marvelling in my mind whether I could really bear to see him dying slowly of starvation with that savoury pie tantalizingly under his nose. The crash which I had heard a few minutes ago prepared me for a change of scene. Even so, I confess that the sight which I beheld glued me to the threshold. There sat Theodore at the table, finishing the last morsel of pie, whilst the chair-bedstead lay in a tangled heap upon the floor.

I cannot tell you how nasty he was to me about the whole thing, although I showed myself at once ready to forgive him all his lies and his treachery, and was at great pains to explain to him how I had given up my own bed and strapped him into it solely for the benefit of his health, seeing that at the moment he was threatened with delirium tremens.

He would not listen to reason or to the most elementary dictates of friendship. Having poured the vials of his bilious temper over my devoted head, he became as perverse and as obstinate as a mule. With the most consummate impudence I ever beheld in any human being, he flatly denied all knowledge of the bracelet.

Whilst I talked he stalked past me into the ante-chamber, where he at once busied himself in collecting all his goods and chattels. These he stuffed into his pockets until he appeared to be bulging all over his ugly-body; then he went to the door ready to go out. On the threshold he turned and gave me a supercilious glance over his shoulder.

"Take note, my good Ratichon," he said, "that our partnership is dissolved as from to-morrow, the twentieth day of September."

"As from this moment, you infernal scoundrel!" I cried.

But he did not pause to listen, and slammed the door in my face.

For two or three minutes I remained quite still, whilst I heard the shuffling footsteps slowly descending the corridor. Then I followed him, quietly, surreptitiously, as a fox will follow its prey. He never turned round once, but obviously he knew that he was being followed.

I will not weary you, my dear Sir, with the details of the dance which he led me in and about Paris during the whole of that memorable day. Never a morsel passed my lips from breakfast to long after sundown. He tried every trick known to the profession to throw me off the scent. But I stuck to him like a leech. When he sauntered I sauntered; when he ran I ran; when he glued his nose to the window of an eating house I halted under a doorway close by; when he went to sleep on a bench in the Luxembourg Gardens I watched over him as a mother over a babe.

Towards evening—it was an hour after sunset and the street-lamps were just being lighted—he must have thought that he had at last got rid of me; for, after looking carefully behind him, he suddenly started to walk much faster and with an amount of determination which he had lacked hitherto. I marvelled if he was not making for the Rue Daunou, where was situated the squalid tavern of ill-fame which he was wont to frequent. I was not mistaken.

I tracked the traitor to the corner of the street, and saw him disappear beneath the doorway of the Taverne des Trois Tigres. I resolved to follow. I had money in my pocket—about twenty-five sous—and I was mightily thirsty. I started to run down the street, when suddenly Theodore came rushing back out of the tavern, hatless and breathless, and before I succeeded in dodging him he fell into my arms.

"My money!" he said hoarsely. "I must have my money at once! You thief! You . . ."

Once again my presence of mind stood me in good stead.

"Pull yourself together, Theodore," I said with much dignity, "and do not make a scene in the open street."

But Theodore was not at all prepared to pull himself together. He was livid with rage.

"I had five francs in my pocket last night!" he cried. "You have stolen them, you abominable rascal!"

"And you stole from me a bracelet worth three thousand francs to the firm," I retorted. "Give me that bracelet and you shall have your money back."

"I can't," he blurted out desperately.

"How do you mean, you can't?" I exclaimed, whilst a horrible fear like an icy claw suddenly gripped at my heart. "You haven't lost it, have you?"

"Worse!" he cried, and fell up against me in semi-unconsciousness.

I shook him violently. I bellowed in his ear, and suddenly, after that one moment of apparent unconsciousness, he became, not only wide awake, but as strong as a lion and as furious as a bull. We closed in on one another. He hammered at me with his fists, calling me every kind of injurious name he could think of, and I had need of all my strength to ward off his attacks.

For a few moments no one took much notice of us. Fracas and quarrels outside the drinking-houses in the mean streets of Paris were so frequent these days that the police did not trouble much about them. But after a while Theodore became so violent that I was forced to call vigorously for help. I thought he meant to murder me. People came rushing out of the tavern, and someone very officiously started whistling for the gendarmes. This had the effect of bringing Theodore to his senses. He calmed down visibly, and before the crowd had had time to collect round us we had both sauntered off, walking in apparent amity side by side down the street.

But at the first corner Theodore halted, and this time he confined himself to gripping me by the arm with one hand whilst with the other he grasped one of the buttons of my coat.

"That five francs," he said in a hoarse, half-choked voice. "I must have that five francs! Can't you see that I can't have that bracelet till I have my five francs wherewith to redeem it?"

"To redeem it!" I gasped. I was indeed glad then that he held me by the arm, for it seemed to me as if I was falling down a yawning abyss which had opened at my feet.

"Yes," said Theodore, and his voice sounded as if it came from a great distance and through cotton-wool,

"I knew that you would be after that bracelet like a famished hyena after a bone, so I tied it securely inside the pocket of the blouse I was wearing, and left this with Legros, the landlord of the Trois Tigres. It was a good blouse; he lent me five francs on it. Of course, he knew nothing about the bracelet then. But he only lends money to clients in this manner on the condition that it is repaid within twenty-four hours. I have got to pay him back before eight o'clock this evening or he will dispose of the blouse as he thinks best. It is close on eight o'clock now. Give me back my five francs, you confounded thief, before Legros has time to discover the bracelet! We'll share the reward, I promise you. Faith of an honest man. You liar, you cheat, you—"

What was the use of talking? I had not got five francs. I had spent ten sous in getting myself some breakfast, and three francs in a savoury pie flavoured with garlic and in a quarter of a bottle of cognac. I groaned aloud. I had exactly twenty-five sous left.

We went back to the tavern hoping against hope that Legros had not yet turned out the pockets of the blouse, and that we might induce him, by threat or cajolery or the usurious interest of twenty-five sous, to grant his client a further twenty-four hours wherein to redeem the pledge.

One glance at the interior of the tavern, however, told us that all our hopes were in vain. Legros, the landlord, was even then turning the blouse over and over, whilst his hideous hag of a wife was talking to the police inspector, who was showing her the paper that announced the offer of two thousand five hundred francs for the recovery of a valuable bracelet, the property of Mlle. Mars, the distinguished tragedienne.

We only waited one minute with our noses glued against the windows of the Trois Tigres, just long enough to see Legros extracting the leather case from the pocket of the blouse, just long enough to hear the police inspector saying peremptorily:

"You, Legros, ought to be able to let the police know who stole the bracelet. You must know who left that blouse with you last night."

Then we both fled incontinently down the street.

Now, Sir, was I not right when I said that honour and loyalty are the essential qualities in our profession? If Theodore had not been such a liar and such a traitor, he and I, between us, would have been richer by three thousand francs that day.

CHAPTER VII

AN OVER-SENSITIVE HEART

1.

No doubt, Sir, that you have noticed during the course of our conversations that Nature has endowed me with an over-sensitive heart. I feel keenly, Sir, very keenly. Blows dealt me by Fate, or, as has been more often the case, by the cruel and treacherous hand of man, touch me on the raw. I suffer acutely. I am highly strung. I am one of those rare beings whom Nature pre-ordained for love and for happiness. I am an ideal family man.

What? You did not know that I was married? Indeed, Sir, I am. And though Madame Ratichon does not perhaps fulfil all my ideals of exquisite womanhood, nevertheless she has been an able and willing helpmate during these last years of comparative prosperity. Yes, you see me fairly prosperous now. My industry, my genius—if I may so express myself—found their reward at last. You will be the first to acknowledge—you, the confidant of my life's history—that that reward was fully deserved. I worked for it, toiled and thought and struggled, up to the last; and had Fate been just, rather than grudging, I should have attained that ideal which would have filled my cup of happiness to the brim.

But, anyway, the episode connected with my marriage did mark the close of my professional career, and is therefore worthy of record. Since that day, Sir—a happy one for me, a blissful one for Mme. Ratichon—I have been able, thanks to the foresight of an all-wise Providence, to gratify my bucolic tastes. I live now, Sir, amidst my flowers, with my dog and my canary and Mme. Ratichon, smiling with kindly indulgence on the struggles and the blunders of my younger colleagues, oft consulted by them in matters that require special tact and discretion. I sit and dream now beneath the shade of a vine-clad arbour of those glorious days of long ago, when kings and emperors placed the destiny of their inheritance in my hands, when autocrats and dictators came to me for assistance and advice, and the name of Hector Ratichon stood for everything that was most astute and most discreet. And if at times a gentle sigh of regret escapes my lips, Mme. Ratichon—whose thinness is ever my despair, for I admire comeliness, Sir, as being more womanly—Mme. Ratichon, I say, comes to me with the gladsome news that dinner is served; and though she is not all that I could wish in the matter of the culinary arts, yet she can fry a cutlet passably, and one of her brothers is a wholesale wine merchant of excellent reputation.

It was soon after my connexion with that abominable Marquis de Firmin-Latour that I first made the acquaintance of the present Mme. Ratichon, under somewhat peculiar circumstances.

I remember it was on the first day of April in the year 1817 that M. Rochez—Fernand Rochez was his exact name—came to see me at my office in the Rue Daunou, and the date proved propitious, as you will presently see. How M. Rochez came to know of my gifts and powers, I cannot tell you. He never would say. He had heard of me through a friend, was all that he vouchsafed to say.

Theodore had shown him in. Ah! have I not mentioned the fact that I had forgiven Theodore his lies and his treachery, and taken him back to my bosom and to my board? My sensitive heart had again got the better of my prudence, and Theodore was installed once more in the antechamber of my apartments in the Rue Daunou, and was, as heretofore, sharing with me all the good things that I could afford. So there he was on duty on that fateful first of April which was destined to be the turning-point of my destiny. And he showed M. de Rochez in.

At once I knew my man—the type, I mean. Immaculately dressed, scented and befrilled, haughty of manner and nonchalant of speech, M. Rochez had the word "adventurer" writ all over his well-groomed person. He was young, good-looking, his nails were beautifully polished, his pantaloons fitted him without a wrinkle. These were of a soft putty shade; his coat was bottle-green, and his hat of the latest modish shape. A perfect exquisite, in fact.

And he came to the point without much preamble.

"M.—er—Ratichon," he said, "I have heard of you through a friend, who tells me that you are the most unscrupulous scoundrel he has ever come across."

"Sir—!" I began, rising from my seat in indignant protest at the coarse insult. But with an authoritative gesture he checked the flow of my indignation.

"No comedy, I pray you, Sir," he said. "We are not at the Theatre Molière, but, I presume, in an office where business is transacted both briefly and with discretion."

"At your service, Monsieur," I replied.

"Then listen, will you?" he went on curtly, "and pray do not interrupt. Only speak in answer to a question from me."

I bowed my head in silence. Thus must the proud suffer when they happen to be sparsely endowed with riches.

"You have no doubt heard of Mlle. Goldberg," M. Rochez continued after a moment's pause, "the lovely daughter of the rich usurer in the Rue des Médecins."

I had heard of Mlle. Goldberg. Her beauty and her father's wealth were reported to be fabulous. I indicated my knowledge of the beautiful lady by a mute inclination of the head.

"I love Mlle. Goldberg," my client resumed, "and I have reason for the belief that I am not altogether indifferent to her. Glances, you understand, from eyes as expressive as those of the exquisite Jewess speak more eloquently than words."

He had forbidden me to speak, so I could only express concurrence in the sentiments which he expressed by a slight elevation of my left eyebrow.

"I am determined to win the affections of Mlle. Goldberg," M. Rochez went on glibly, "and equally am I determined to make her my wife."

"A very natural determination," I remarked involuntarily.

"My only trouble with regard to pressing my court is the fact that my lovely Leah is never allowed outside her father's house, save in his company or that of his sister—an old maid of dour mien and sour disposition, who acts the part of a duenna with dog-like tenacity. Over and over again have I tried to approach the lady of my heart, only to be repelled or roughly rebuked for my insolence by her irascible old aunt."

"You are not the first lover, Sir," I remarked drily, "who hath seen obstacles thus thrown in his way, and—"

"One moment, M.—er—Ratichon," he broke in sharply. "I have not finished. I will not attempt to describe my feelings to you. I have been writhing—yes, writhing!—in face of those obstacles of which you speak so lightly, and for a long time I have been cudgelling my brains as to the possible means whereby I might approach my divinity unchecked. Then one day I bethought me of you—"

"Of me, Sir?" I ejaculated, sorely puzzled. "Why of me?"

"None of my friends," he replied nonchalantly, "would care to undertake so scrubby a task as I would assign to you."

"I pray you to be more explicit," I retorted with unimpaired dignity.

Once more he paused. Obviously he was a born mountebank, and he calculated all his effects to a nicety.

"You, M.—er—Ratichon," he said curtly at last, "will have to take the duenna off my hands."

I was beginning to understand. So I let him prattle on the while my busy brain was already at work evolving the means to render this man service, which in its turn I expected to be amply repaid. Thus I cannot repeat exactly all that he said, for I was only listening with half an ear. But the substance of it all was this: I was to pose as the friend of M. Fernand Rochez, and engage the attention of Mlle. Goldberg senior the while he paid his court to the lovely Leah. It was not a repellent task altogether, because M. Rochez's suggestion opened a vista of pleasant parties at open-air cafés, with foaming tankards of beer, on warm afternoons the while the young people sipped sirops and fed on love. My newly found friend was pleased to admit that my personality and appearance would render my courtship of the elderly duenna a comparatively easy one. She would soon, he declared, fall a victim to my charms.

After which the question of remuneration came in, and over this we did not altogether agree. Ultimately I decided to accept an advance of two hundred francs and a new suit of clothes, which I at once declared was indispensable under the circumstances, seeing that in my well-worn coat I might have the appearance of a fortune-hunter in the eyes of the suspicious old dame.

Within my mind I envisaged the possibility of touching M. Rochez for a further two hundred francs if and when opportunity arose.

2.

The formal introduction took place on the boulevards one fine afternoon shortly after that. Mlle. Leah was walking under the trees with her duenna when we—M. Rochez and I—came face to face with them. My friend raised his hat, and I did likewise. Mademoiselle Leah blushed and the ogre frowned. Sir, she was an ogre!—bony and angular and hook-nosed, with thin lips that closed with a snap, and cold grey eyes that sent a shiver down your spine! Rochez introduced me to her, and I made myself exceedingly agreeable to her, while my friend succeeded in exchanging two or three whispered words with his inamorata.

But we did not get very far that day. Mlle. Goldberg senior soon marched her lovely charge away.

Ah, Sir, she was lovely indeed! And in my heart I not only envied Rochez his good fortune but I also felt how entirely unworthy he was of it. Nor did the beautiful Leah give me the impression of being quite so deeply struck with his charms as he would have had me believe. Indeed, it struck me during those few minutes that I stood dutifully talking to her duenna that the fair young Jewess cast more than one approving glance in my direction.

Be that as it may, the progress of our respective courtships, now that the ice was broken, took on a more decided turn. At first it only amounted to meetings on the boulevards and a cursory greeting, but soon Mlle. Goldberg senior, delighted with my conversation, would deliberately turn to walk with me under the trees the while Fernand Rochez followed by the side of his adored. A week later the ladies accepted my friend's offer to sit under the awning of the Café Bourbon and to sip sirops, whilst we indulged in tankards of foaming "blondes."

Within a fortnight, Sir—I may say it without boasting—I had Mlle. Goldberg senior in the hollow of my hand. On the boulevards, as soon as she caught sight of me, her dour face would be wreathed in smiles, a row of large yellow teeth would appear between her thin lips, and her cold, grey eyes would soften with a glance of welcome which more than ever sent a cold shudder down my spine. While we four were together, either promenading or sitting at open-air cafés in the cool of the evening, the old duenna had eyes and ears only for me, and if my friend Rochez did not get on with his own courtship as fast as he would have wished the fault rested entirely with him.

For he did *not* get on with his courtship, and that was a fact. The fair Leah was very sweet, very coy, greatly amused, I fancy, at her aunt's obvious infatuation for me, and not a little flattered at the handsome M. Rochez's attentions to herself. But there it all ended. And whenever I questioned Rochez on the subject, he flew into a temper and consigned all middle-aged Jewesses to perdition, and all the lovely and young ones to a comfortable kind of Hades to which he alone amongst the male sex would have access. From which I gathered that I was not wrong in my surmises, that the fair Leah had been smitten by my personality and my appearance rather than by those of my friend, and that he was suffering the pangs of an insane jealousy.

This, of course, he never would admit. All that he told me one day was that Leah, with the characteristic timidity of her race, refused to marry him unless she could obtain her father's consent to the union. Old Goldberg, duly approached on the matter, flatly forbade his daughter to have anything further to do with that fortune-hunter, that parasite, that beggarly pick-thank—such, Sir, were but a few complimentary epithets which he hurled with great volubility at his daughter's absent suitor.

It was from Mlle. Goldberg, senior, that my friend and I had the details of that stormy interview between father and daughter; after which, she declared that interviews between the lovers would necessarily become very difficult of arrangement. From which you will gather that the worthy soul, though she was as ugly as sin, was by this time on the side of the angels. Indeed, she was more than that. She professed herself willing to aid and abet them in every way she could. This Rochez confided to me, together with his assurance that he was determined to take his Fate into his own hands and, since the beautiful Leah would not come to him of her own accord, to carry her off by force.

Ah, my dear Sir, those were romantic days, you must remember! Days when men placed the possession of the woman they loved above every treasure, every consideration upon earth. Ah, romance! Romance, Sir, was the breath of our nostrils, the blood in our veins! Imagine how readily we all fell in with my friend's plans. I, of course, was the moving spirit in it all; mine was the genius which was destined to turn gilded romance into grim reality. Yes, grim! For you shall see! . . .

Mlle. Goldberg, senior, who appropriately enough was named Sarah, gave us the clue how to proceed, after which my genius worked alone.

You must know that old Goldberg's house in the Rue des Médecins—a large apartment house in which he occupied a few rooms on the ground floor behind his shop—backed on to a small uncultivated garden which ended in a tall brick wall, the meeting-place of all the felines in the neighbourhood, and in which there was a small postern gate, now disused. This gate gave on a narrow cul-de-sac—grandiloquently named Passage Corneille—which was flanked on the opposite side by the tall boundary wall of an adjacent convent.

That cul-de-sac was marked out from the very first in my mind as our objective. Around and about it, as it were, did I build the edifice of my schemes, aided by the ever-willing Sarah. The old maid threw herself into the affair with zest, planning and contriving like a veritable strategist; and I must admit that she was full of resource and invention. We were now in mid-May and enjoying a spell of hot summer weather. This gave the inventive Sarah the excuse for using the back garden as a place wherein to sit in the cool of the evening in the company of her niece.

Ah, you see the whole thing now at a glance, do you not? The postern gate, the murky night, the daring lover, the struggling maiden, the willing accomplices. The actors were all there, ready for the curtain to be rung up on the palpitating drama.

Then it was that a brilliant idea came into my brain. It was born on the very day that I realized with indisputable certainty that the lovely Leah was not in reality in love with Rochez. He fatuously believed that she was ready to fall into his arms, that only maidenly timidity held her back, and that the moment she had been snatched from her father's house and found herself in the arms of her adoring lover, she would turn to him in the very fullness of love and confidence.

But I knew better. I had caught a look now and again—an undefinable glance, which told me the whole pitiable tale. She did not love Rochez; and in the drama which we were preparing to enact the curtain would fall on his rapture and her unhappiness.

Ah, Sir! imagine what my feelings were when I realized this! This fair girl, against whom we were all conspiring like so many traitors, was still ignorant of the fatal brink on which she stood. She chatted and coquetted and smiled, little dreaming that in a very few days her happiness would be wrecked and she would be linked for life to a man whom she could never love. Rochez's idea, of course, was primarily to get hold of her fortune. I had already ascertained for him, through the ever-willing Sarah, that this fortune came from Leah's grandfather, who had left a sum of two hundred thousand francs on trust for her children, she to enjoy the income for her life. There certainly was a clause in the will whereby the girl would forfeit that fortune if she married without her father's consent; but according to Rochez's plans this could scarcely be withheld once she had been taken forcibly away from home, held in durance, and with her reputation hopelessly compromised. She could then pose as an injured victim, throw herself at her father's feet, and beg him to give that consent without which she would for ever remain an outcast of society, a pariah amongst her kind.

A pretty piece of villainous combination, you will own! And I, Sir, was to lend a hand in this abomination!—nay, I was to be the chief villain in the drama! It was I who, even now, was spending the hours of the night, when I might have been dreaming sentimental dreams, in oiling the lock of the postern gate which was to give us access into papa Goldberg's garden. It was I who, under cover of darkness and guided by that old jade Sarah, was to sneak into that garden on the appointed night and forcibly seize the unsuspecting maiden and carry her to the carriage which Rochez would have in readiness for her.

You see what a coward he was! It was a criminal offence in those days, punishable with deportation to New Caledonia, to abduct a young lady from her parents' house; and Rochez left me the dirty work to do in case the girl screamed and attracted the police. Now you will tell me if I was not justified in doing what I did, and I will abide by your judgment.

I was to take all the risks, remember!—New Caledonia, the police, the odium attached to so foul a deed; and do you know for what? For a paltry thousand francs, which with much difficulty I had induced Rochez—nay, forced him!—to hand over to me in anticipation of what I was about to accomplish for his sake. A thousand francs! Did this miserliness not characterize the man? Was it to such a scrubby knave that I, at risk of my life and of my honour, would hand over that jewel amongst women, that pearl above price?—a lady with a personal fortune amounting to two hundred thousand francs?

No, Sir; I would not! Then and there I vowed that I would not! Mine were to be all the risks; then mine should be the reward! What Rochez meant to do, that I could too, and with far greater reason. The lovely Leah did at times frown on Fernand; but she invariably smiled on me. She would fall into my arms far more readily than into his, and papa Goldberg would be equally forced to give his consent to her marriage with me as with that self-seeking carpet-knight whom he abhorred.

Needless to say, I kept my own counsel, and did not speak of my project even to Sarah. To all appearances I was to be the mere tool in this affair, the unfortunate cat employed to snatch the roast chestnuts out of the fire for the gratification of a mealy-mouthed monkey.

3.

The appointed day and hour were at hand. Fernand Rochez had engaged a barouche which was to take him and his lovely victim to a little house at Auteuil, which he had rented for the purpose. There the lovers were to lie perdu until such time as papa Goldberg had relented and the marriage could be duly solemnized in the synagogue of the Rue des Halles. Sarah had offered in the meanwhile to do all that in her power lay to soften the old man's heart and to bring about the happy conclusion of the romantic adventure.

For the latter we had chosen the night of May 23rd. It was a moonless night, and the Passage Corneille, from whence I was to operate, was most usefully dark. Sarah Goldberg had, according to convention, left the postern gate on the latch, and at ten o'clock precisely I made my way up the cul-de-sac and cautiously turned the handle of the door. I confess that my heart beat somewhat uncomfortably in my bosom.

I had left Rochez and his barouche in the Rue des Pipots, about a hundred metres from the angle of the Passage Corneille, and it was along those hundred metres of a not altogether unfrequented street that he expected me presently to carry a possibly screaming and struggling burden in the very teeth of a gendarmerie always on the look-out for exciting captures.

No, Sir; that was not to be! And it was with a resolute if beating heart that I presently felt the postern gate yielding to the pressure of my hand. The neighbouring church clock of St. Sulpice had just finished striking ten. I pushed open the gate and tip-toed across the threshold.

In the garden the boughs of a dilapidated old ash tree were soughing in the wind above my head, whilst from the top of the boundary wall the yarring and yowling of beasts of the feline species grated unpleasantly on my ear. I could not see my hand before my eyes, and had just stretched it out in order to guide my footsteps when it was seized with a kindly yet firm pressure, whilst a voice murmured softly:

"Hush!"

"Who is it?" I whispered in response.

"It is I—Sarah!" the voice replied. "Everything is all right, but Leah is unsuspecting. I am sure that if she suspected anything she would not set foot outside the door."

"What shall we do?" I asked.

"Wait here a moment quietly," Sarah rejoined, speaking in a rapid whisper, "under cover of this wall. Within the next few minutes Leah will come out of the house. I have left my knitting upon a garden chair, and I will ask her to run out and fetch it. That will be your opportunity. The chair is in the angle of the wall, there," she added, pointing to her right, "not three paces from where you are standing now. Leah has a white dress on. She will have to stoop in order to pick up the knitting. I have taken the precaution to entangle the wool in the leg of the chair, so she will be some few seconds entirely at your mercy. Have you a shawl?"

I had, of course, provided myself with one. A shawl is always a necessary adjunct to such adventures. Breathlessly, silently, I intimated to my kind accomplice that I would obey her behests and that I was prepared for every eventuality. The next moment her hold upon my hand relaxed, she gave another quickly-whispered "Hush!" and disappeared into the night.

For a second or two after that my ear caught the soft sound of her retreating footsteps, then nothing more. To say that I felt anxious and ill at ease was but to put it mildly. I was face to face with an adventure which might cost me at least five years' acute discomfort in New Caledonia, but which might also bring me as rich a reward as could befall any man of modest ambitions: a lovely wife and a comfortable fortune. My whole life seemed to be hanging on a thread, and my overwrought senses seemed almost to catch the sound of the spinning-wheel of Fate weaving the web of my destiny.

A moment or two later I again caught the distinct sound of a gentle footfall upon the soft earth. My eyes by now were somewhat accustomed to the gloom. It was very dark, you understand; but through the darkness I saw something white moving slowly toward me. Then my heart thumped more furiously than ever before. I dared not breathe. I saw the lovely Leah approaching, or, rather, I felt her approach, for it was too dark to see. She moved in the direction which Sarah had indicated to me as being the place where stood the garden chair with the knitting upon it. I grasped the shawl. I was ready.

Another few seconds of agonising suspense went by. The fair Leah had ceased to move. Undoubtedly she was engaged in disentangling the wool from the leg of the chair. That was my opportunity. More stealthy than any cat, I tiptoed toward the chair—and, indeed, at that moment I blessed the sudden yowl set up by some feline in its wrath which rent the still night air and effectually drowned any sound which I might make.

There, not three paces away from me, was the dim outline of the young girl's form vaguely discernible in the gloom—a white mass, almost motionless, against a background of inky blackness. With a quick intaking of my breath I sprang forward, the shawl outspread in my hand, and with a quick dexterous gesture I threw it over her head, and the next second had her, faintly struggling, in my arms. She was as light as a feather, and I was as strong as a giant. Think of it, Sir! There was I, alone in the darkness, holding in my arms, together with a lovely form, a fortune of two hundred thousand francs!

Of that fool Fernand Rochez I did not trouble to think. He had a barouche waiting *up* the Rue des Pipots, a hundred metres from the corner of the Passage Corneille, but I had a chaise and pair of horses waiting *down* that same street, and that now was my objective. Yes, Sir! I had arranged the whole thing! But I had done it for mine own advantage, not for that of the miserly friend who had been too great a coward to risk his own skin for the sake of his beloved.

The guerdon was mine, and I was determined this time that no traitor or ingrate should filch from me the reward of my labours. With the thousand francs which Rochez had given me for my services I had engaged the chaise and horses, paid the coachman lavishly, and secured a cosy little apartment for my future wife in a pleasant hostelry I knew of at Suresnes.

I had taken the precaution to leave the wicket-gate on the latch. With my foot I pushed it open, and, keeping well under the cover of the tall convent wall, I ran swiftly to the corner of the Rue des Pipots. Here I paused a moment. Through the silence of the night my ear caught the faint sound of horses snorting and harness jingling in the distance, both sides from where I stood; but of gendarmes or passers-by there was no sign. Gathering up the full measure of my courage and holding my precious burden closer to my heart, I ran quickly down the street.

Within the next few seconds I had the seemingly inanimate maiden safely deposited in the inside of the barouche and myself sitting by her side. The driver cracked his whip, and whilst I, happy but exhausted, was mopping my streaming forehead the chaise rattled gaily along the uneven pavements of the great city in the direction of Suresnes.

What that fool Rochez was doing I could not definitely ascertain. I looked through the vasistas of the coach, but could see nothing in pursuit of us. Then I turned my full attention to my lovely companion. It was pitch dark inside the carriage, you understand; only from time to time, as we drove past an overhanging street lanthorn, I caught a glimpse of that priceless bundle beside me, which lay there so still and so snug, still wrapped up in the shawl.

With cautious, loving fingers I undid its folds. Under cover of the darkness the sweet and modest creature, released of her bonds, turned for an instant to me, and for a few, very few, happy seconds I held her in my arms.

"Have no fear, fair one," I murmured in her ear. "It is I, Hector Ratichon, who adores you and who cannot live without you! Forgive me for this seeming violence, which was prompted by an undying passion, and remember that to me you are as sacred as a divinity until the happy hour when I can proclaim you to the world as my beloved wife!"

I pressed her against my heart, and my lips imprinted a delicate kiss upon her forehead. After which, with chaste decorum, she once more turned away from me, covered her face and head with the shawl, and drew back into the remote corner of the carriage, where she remained, silent and absorbed, no doubt, in the contemplation of her happiness.

I respected her silence, and I, too, fell to meditating upon my good fortune. Here was I, Sir, within sight of a haven wherein I could live through the twilight of my days in comfort and in peace, a beautiful young wife, a modest fortune! I had never in my wildest dreams envisaged a Fate more fair. The little house at Chantilly which I coveted, the plot of garden, the espalier peaches—all, all would be mine now! It seemed indeed too good to be true!

The very next moment I was rudely awakened from those golden dreams by a loud clatter, and stern voices shouting the ominous word, "Halt!" The carriage drew up with such a jerk that I was flung off my seat against the front window and my nose seriously bruised. A faint cry of terror came from the precious bundle beside me.

"Have no fear, my beloved," I whispered hurriedly. "Your own Hector will protect you!"

Already the door of the carriage had been violently torn open; the next moment a gruff voice called out peremptorily:

"By order of the Chief Commissary of Police!"

I was dumbfounded. In what manner had the Chief Commissary of Police been already apprised of this affair? The whole thing was, of course, a swift and vengeful blow dealt to me by that cowardly Rochez. But how, in the name of thunder, had he got to work so quickly? But, of course, there was no time now for reflection. The gruff voice was going on more peremptorily and more insistently:

"Is Hector Ratichon here?"

I was dumb. My throat had closed up, and I could not have uttered a sound to save my life. The police had even got my name quite straight!

"Now then, Ratichon," that same irascible voice continued, "get out of there! In the name of the law I charge you with the abduction of a defenceless female, and my orders are to bring you forthwith before the Chief Commissary of Police."

Then it was, Sir, that bliss once more re-entered my soul. I had just felt a small hand pressing something crisp into mine, whilst a soft voice whispered in my ear:

"Give him this, and tell him to let you go in peace. Say that I am Mademoiselle Goldberg, your promised wife."

The feel of that crackling note in my hand at once restored my courage. Covering the lovely creature beside me with a protecting arm, I replied boldly to the minion of the law.

"This lady," I said, "is my affianced wife. You, Sir Gendarme, are overstepping your powers. I demand that you let us proceed in peace."

"My orders are—" the gendarme resumed; but already my sensitive ear had detected a faint wavering in the gruffness of his voice. The hectoring tone had gone out of it. I could not see him, of course, but somehow I felt that his attitude had become less arrogant and his glance more shifty.

"This gentleman has spoken the truth," now came in soft, dulcet tones from under the shawl that wrapped the head of my beloved. "I am Mlle. Goldberg, M. le Gendarme, and I am travelling with M. Hector Ratichon entirely of my own free will, since I have promised him that I would be his wife."

"Ah!" the gendarme ejaculated, obviously mollified.

"If Mademoiselle is the fiancée of Monsieur, and is acting of her own free will—"

"It is not for you to interfere, eh, my friend?" I broke in jocosely. "You will now let us proceed in peace, and for your trouble you will no doubt accept this token of my consideration." And, groping in the darkness, I found the rough hand of the gendarme, and speedily pressed into it the crisp note which my adored one had given to me.

"Ah!" he said, with very obvious gratification. "If Monsieur Ratichon will assure me that Mademoiselle here is indeed his affianced wife, then indeed it is not a case of abduction, and—"

"Abduction!" I retorted, flaring up in righteous indignation. "Who dares to use the word in connexion with this lovely lady? Mademoiselle Goldberg, I swear, will be Madame Ratichon within the next four and twenty hours. And the sooner you, Sir Gendarme, allow us to proceed on our way the less pain will you cause to this distressed and virtuous damsel."

This settled the whole affair quite comfortably. The gendarme shut the carriage door with a bang, and at my request gave the order to the driver to proceed. The latter once again cracked his whip, and once again the cumbrous vehicle, after an awkward lurch, rattled on its way along the cobblestones of the sleeping city.

Once more I was alone with the priceless treasure by my side—alone and happy—more happy, I might say, than I had been before. Had not my adored one openly acknowledged her love for me and her desire to stand with me at the hymeneal altar? To put it vulgarly—though vulgarity in every form is repellent to me—she had burnt her boats. She had allowed her name to be coupled with mine in the presence of the minions of the law. What, after that, could her father do but give his consent to a union which alone would save his only child's reputation from the cruelty of waggish tongues?

No doubt, Sir, that I was happy. True, that when the uncouth gendarme finally slammed to the door of our carriage and we restarted on our way, my ears had been unpleasantly tickled by the sound of prolonged and ribald laughter— laughter which sounded strangely and unpleasantly familiar. But after a few seconds' serious reflection I dismissed the matter from my thoughts. If, as indeed I gravely suspected, it was Fernand Rochez who had striven thus to put a spoke in the wheel of my good fortune, he would certainly not have laughed when I drove triumphantly away with my conquered bride by my side. And, of course, my ears *must* have deceived me when they caught the sound of a girl's merry laugh mingling with the more ribald one of the man.

4.

I have paused purposely, Sir, ere I embark upon the narration of the final stage of this, my life's adventure.

The chaise was bowling along the banks of the river toward Suresnes. Presently the driver struck to his right and plunged into the fastnesses of the Bois de Boulogne. For a while, therefore, we were in utter darkness. My lovely companion neither moved nor spoke. Somewhere in the far distance a church clock struck eleven. One whole hour had gone by since first I had embarked on this great undertaking.

I was excited, feverish. The beautiful Leah's silence and tranquillity grated upon my nerves. I could not understand how she could remain there so placid when her whole life's happiness had so suddenly, so unexpectedly, been assured. I became more and more fidgety as time went on. Soon I felt that I could no longer hold myself in proper control. Being of an impulsive disposition, this tranquil acceptance of so great a joy became presently intolerable, and, unable to restrain my ardour any longer, I seized that passive bundle of loveliness in my arms.

"Have no fear," I murmured once again, as I pressed her to my heart.

But my admonition was obviously unnecessary. The beautiful Leah showed not the slightest sign of fear. She rested her head against my shoulder and put one arm around my neck. I was in raptures.

Just then the vehicle swung out of the Bois and once more rattled upon the cobblestones. This time we were nearing Suresnes. A vague light, emanating from the lanthorns at the bridge-head, was already faintly visible ahead of us. Soon it grew brighter. The next moment we passed immediately beneath the lanthorns. The interior of the carriage was flooded with light . . . and, Sir, I gave a gasp of unadulterated dismay! The being whom I held in my arms, whose face was even at that moment raised up to my own, was not the lovely Leah! It was Sarah, Sir! Sarah Goldberg, the dour, angular aunt, whose yellow teeth gleamed for one brief moment through her thin lips as she threw me one of those glances of amorous welcome which invariably sent a cold shiver down my spine. Sarah Goldberg! I scarce could believe my eyes, and for a moment did indeed think that the elusive, swiftly-vanished light of the bridge-head lanthorns had played my excited senses a weird and cruel trick. But no! The very next second proved my disillusionment. Sarah spoke to me!

She spoke to me and laughed! Ah, she was happy, Sir! Happy in that she had completely and irrevocably tricked me! That traitor Fernand Rochez was up to the neck in the plot which had saddled me for ever with an ugly, elderly wife of dour mien and no fortune, while he and the lovely Leah were spinning the threads of perfect love at the other end of Paris and laughing their fill at my discomfiture. Think, Sir, what I suffered during those few brief minutes while the coach lurched through the narrow streets of Suresnes, and I had perforce to listen to the protestations of undying love from this unprepossessing female!

That love, she vowed, was her excuse, and everything, she asserted, was fair in love and war. She knew that after Rochez had attained his heart's desire and carried off the lady of his choice—which he had successfully done half an hour before I myself made my way up the Passage Corneille—I would pass out of her life for ever. This she could not endure. Life at once would become intolerable. And, aided and abetted by Rochez and Leah, she had planned and contrived my mystification and won me by foul means, since she could not do so by fair; and it seemed as if her volubility then was the forecast of what my life with her would be in the future. Talk! Talk! Talk! She never ceased!

She told me the whole story of the abominable conspiracy against my liberty. Her brother, M. Goldberg, she explained, had determined upon remarriage. She, Sarah, felt that henceforth she would be in the way of everybody; she would have no home. Leah married to Rochez; a new and young Mme. Goldberg ruling in the old house of the Rue des Médecins! Ah, it was unthinkable!

And I, Sir—I, Hector Ratichon—had, it appears, by my polite manners and prepossessing ways, induced this dour old maid to believe that she was not altogether indifferent to me. Ah, how I cursed my own charms, when I realised whither they had led me! It seems that it was that fickle jade Leah who first imagined the whole execrable plot. Rochez was to entrust me with the task of carrying off his beloved, and thus I would be tricked in the darkness into abducting Mlle. Goldberg senior from her home. Then some friends of Rochez arranged to play the comedy of false gendarmes, and again I was tricked into acknowledging Sarah as my affianced wife before independent witnesses. After that I could no longer repudiate mine honourable intentions, for if I did, then I should be arraigned before the law on a criminal charge of abduction. In this comedy of false gendarmes Rochez himself and the heartless Leah had joined with zest and laughed over my discomfiture, whilst the friends who played their rôles to such perfection had a paltry hundred francs each as the price of this infamous trick. Now my doom was sealed, and all that was left for me to do was to think disconsolately over my future.

I did bitterly reproach Sarah for her treachery and tried to still her protestations of love by pointing out to her that I had absolutely no fortune, and could only offer her a life of squalor, not to say of what. But this she knew, and vowed that penury by my side would make her happier than luxury beside any other man. Ah, Sir, 'tis given to few men to arouse such selfless passion in a woman's heart, and it hath oft been my dream in the past one day thus to be adored for myself alone!

But for the moment I was too deeply angered to listen placidly to Sarah's vows of undying affection. My nerves were irritated by her fulsome adulation; indeed, I could not bear the sight of her nor yet the sound of her voice. You may imagine how thankful I was when the chaise came at last to a halt outside the humble little hostelry where I had engaged the room which I had so fondly hoped would have been occupied by the lovely and fickle Leah.

I bundled Mlle. Goldberg senior into the house, and here again I had to endure galling mortification in the shape of sidelong glances cast at me and my future bride by the landlord of the hostelry and his ill-bred daughter. When I engaged the room I had very foolishly told them that it would be occupied by a lovely lady who had consented to be my wife, and that she would remain here in happy seclusion until such time as all arrangements for our wedding were complete. The humiliation of these vulgar people's irony seemed like the last straw which overweighed my forbearance. The room and pension I had already paid two days in advance, so I had nothing more to say either to the ribald landlord or to Mlle. Goldberg senior. I was bitterly angered against her, and refused her the solace of a kindly look or of an encouraging pressure from my hand, even though she waited for both with the pathetic patience of an old spaniel.

I re-entered the coach, which was to take me back to mine own humble lodgings in Passy. Here at least I was alone—alone with my gloomy thoughts. My heart was full of wrath against the woman who had so basely tricked me, and I viewed with dismay amounting almost to despair the prospect of spending the rest of my life in her company. That night I slept but little, nor yet the following night, or the night after that. Those days I spent in seclusion, thankful for my solitude.

Twice each day did Mlle. Goldberg come to my lodgings. In the foolish past I had somewhat injudiciously acquainted her of where I lived. Now she came and asked to be allowed to see me, but invariably did I refuse thus to gratify her. I felt that time alone would perhaps soften my feelings a little towards her. In the meanwhile I must commend her discretion and delicacy of procedure. She did not in any way attempt to molest me. When she was told by Theodore— whom I employed during the day to guard me against unwelcome visitors—that I refused to see her, she invariably went away without demur, nor did she refer in any way, either with adjurations or threats, to the impending wedding. Indeed, Sir, she was a lady of vast discretion.

On the third day, however, I received a visit from M. Goldberg himself. I could not refuse to see him. Indeed, he would not be denied, but roughly pushed Theodore aside, who tried to hinder him. He had come armed with a riding-whip, and nothing but mine own innate dignity saved me from outrage. He came, Sir, with a marriage licence for his sister and me in one pocket and with a denunciation to the police against me for abduction in another. He gave me the choice. What could I do, Sir? I was like a helpless babe in the hands of unscrupulous brigands!

The marriage licence was for the following day—at the mairie of the eighth arrondissement first, and in the synagogue of the Rue des Halles afterwards. I chose the marriage licence. What could I do, Sir? I was helpless!

Of my wedding day I have but a dim recollection. It was all hustle and bustle; from the mairie to the synagogue, and thence to the house of M. Goldberg in the Rue des Médecins. I must say that the old usurer received me and my bride with marked amiability. He was, I gathered, genuinely pleased that his sister had found happiness and a home by the side of an honourable man, seeing that he himself was on the point of contracting a fresh alliance with a Jewish lady of unsurpassed loveliness.

Of Rochez and Leah we saw nothing that day, and from one or two words which M. Goldberg let fall I concluded that he was greatly angered against his daughter because of her marriage with a fortune-hunting adventurer, who, he weirdly hinted, had already found quick and exemplary punishment for his crime. I was sincerely glad to hear this, even though I could not get M. Goldberg to explain in what that exemplary punishment consisted.

The climax came at six o'clock of that eventful afternoon, at the hour when I, with the newly-enthroned Mme. Ratichon on my arm, was about to take leave of M. Goldberg. I must admit that at that moment my heart was overflowing with bitterness. I had been led like a lamb to the slaughter; I had been made to look foolish and absurd in the midst of this Israelite community which I despised; I was saddled for the rest of my life with an unprepossessing elderly wife, who could do naught for me but share the penury, the hard crusts, the onion pies with me and Theodore. The only advantage I might ever derive from her was that she would darn my stockings, sew the buttons on my vests, and goffer the frills of my shirts!

Was this not enough to turn any man's naturally sweet disposition to gall? No doubt my mobile face betrayed something of the bitterness of my thoughts, for M. Goldberg at one moment slapped me vigorously on the back and bade me be of good cheer, as things were not so bad as I imagined. I was on the point of asking him what he meant when I saw another gentleman advancing toward me. His face, which was sallow and oily, bore a kind of obsequious smile; his clothes were of rusty black, and his features were markedly Jewish in character. He had some law papers under his arm, and he was perpetually rubbing his thin, bony hands together as if he were for ever washing them.

"Monsieur Hector Ratichon," he said unctuously, "it is with much gratification that I bring you the joyful news."

Joyful news!—to me! Ah, Sir, the words struck at first with cruel irony upon mine ear. But not so a second later, for the Jewish gentleman went on speaking, and what he said appeared to my reeling senses like songs of angels from paradise.

At first I could not grasp his full meaning. A moment ago I had been in the depths of despair, and now—now—a whole vista of beatitude opened out before me! What the worthy Israelite said was that, by the terms of Grandpapa Goldberg's will, if Leah married without her father's consent, one-half of the fortune destined for her would revert to her aunt, Sarah Goldberg, now Madame Hector Ratichon.

Can you wonder that I could scarce believe my ears? One-half that fortune meant that a hundred thousand francs would now become mine! M. Goldberg had already made it very clear to his daughter and to Rochez that he would never give his consent to their marriage, and, as this was now consummated, they had already forfeited one-half of the grandfather's fortune in favour of my

Sarah. That was the exemplary punishment which they were to suffer for their folly.

But their folly—aye! and their treachery—had become my joy. In this moment of heavenly rapture I was speechless, but I turned to Sarah with loving arms outstretched, and the next instant she nestled against my heart like a joyful if elderly bird.

What is said of a people, Sir, is also true of the individual. Happy he who hath no history. Since that never-to-be-forgotten hour my life has run its simple, uneventful course here in this quiet corner of our beautiful France, with my pony and my dog and my chickens, and Mme. Ratichon to minister to my creature comforts.

I bought this little property, Sir, soon after my marriage, and my office in the Rue Daunou knows me no more. You like the house, Sir? Ah, yes! And the garden? . . . After déjeuner you must see my prize chickens. Theodore will show them to you. You did not know Theodore was here? Well, yes! He lives with us. Madame Ratichon finds him useful about the house, and, not being used to luxuries, he is on the whole pleasantly contented.

Ah, here comes Madame Ratichon to tell us that the déjeuner is served! This way, Sir, under the porch. . . . After you!

THE END

Echo Library
www.echo-library.com

Echo Library uses advanced digital print-on-demand technology to build and preserve an exciting world class collection of rare and out-of-print books, making them readily available for everyone to enjoy.

Situated just yards from Teddington Lock on the River Thames, Echo Library was founded in 2005 by Tom Cherrington, a specialist dealer in rare and antiquarian books with a passion for literature.

Please visit our website for a complete catalogue of our books, which includes foreign language titles.

The Right to Read

Echo Library actively supports the Royal National Institute of the Blind's Right to Read initiative by publishing a comprehensive range of large print and clear print titles.

Large Print titles are in 16 point Tiresias font as recommended by the RNIB.

Clear Print titles are in 13 point Tiresias font and designed for those who find standard print difficult to read.

Customer Service

If there is a serious error in the text or layout please send details to feedback@echo-library.com and we will supply a corrected copy. If there is a printing fault or the book is damaged please refer to your supplier.

Printed in the United States
73592LV00003B/83

9 781406 835830